In Those We Trust

only they can betray us

Gloria Grayson

PublishAmerica
Baltimore

First printing

ISBN: 1-4137-4438-9
PUBLISHED BY PUBLISHAMERICA, LLLP
www.publishamerica.com
Baltimore

Printed in the United States of America

A Labor of Love
For My Children

Acknowledgements

Buffy for always believing in me no matter what, during many forms of "overload" and for his perseverance when everything seemed so daunting.

Dr. D. whose patience, caring and understanding over many years made my difficult world an easier place to be.

D.D. for becoming my friend and always listening to me even when I babbled.

Steve for his patience and editing while I nattered in his ear.

Marsky and her mother for their unwavering support and friendship.

Sallad for becoming a trusted friend.

Attorney-at-Law and Notary, D. for being the "straight talker" he is.

V.B. who always goes beyond the call of duty being the caring person and friend she is.

E.F. for her dedication in trying to help me see The Truth.

C.M. and T. for their professional support and encouragement when few others would listen.

My children's "guardian" for keeping my secret and always remaining my friend.

Gary for being a "straight shooter" whose unwavering high moral standards made this book a possibility.

Last but far from the least, Drägo. When you warned me that life with you would be a helluva run I wouldn't listen. Neither of us could have ever imagined the horrific outcome. You have the sequel to this book in the pages of your mind. Tell it, as only you know it. I'm sorry but you gave me no choice.

Chapter One

"If I had walked out here and seen a patrol car and uniforms, I would have turned around and walked right back into the apartment building as if I hadn't even seen you guys," Sandra snapped.

She had just made her way into an unmarked police vehicle occupied by two officers from the local Head Quarters. Two canes assisted her awkward gait over the ice and snow. She recently had both hips and knees replaced due to deterioration from rheumatoid arthritis. It was a gray but mild day in March that showed promise of an early spring. As mild as it was a damp mist chilled the air seeping into her several remaining arthritic joints. Another chill unnoticed by anyone else engulfed her entire being.

"No, we've both been there and done that. We will never be in uniform or patrol car again. We are detectives," Bill said as he assisted her into the car.

Sandra noted the pride in his eyes and voice as he made that claim. Sandra felt sure the man had worked hard to get into his position and deserved to be proud of it.

I'm happy for you, she thought, turning a half-hearted smile in his direction as she settled into the back seat of the car.

"Did anyone think to bring a camera?" she inquired, almost as a thought spoken out loud.

"No," a dull sounding response was heard from the front seat.

"Well you might wish one of you had before this trip is over," she said.

The rest of her opinion went unspoken, your loss.

A new chill shivered its way up her spine.

Sandra was having difficulty concentrating on what was being said by the detectives in the car. Most of it was mumbling in cop lingo anyway so her mind wandered off into its own uncertain world.

Thinking back, Sandra had told the police weeks before that she would not take them on the trip until they got Drägo off the streets. It was her way of holding an ace and staying alive. When she agreed to go on the trip she knew that Drägo was some hundreds of miles away. That only meant that he was off the streets in the immediate area. Sandra hoped the mission she was on would help to speed up the entire process.

Drägo had received a letter from Immigration officials requesting his presence at a meeting, right pronto. That scared him because he didn't have citizenship. Born in Europe he was five when he arrived in North America. Citizenship papers had never been applied for until he was in his late thirties with a scroll of a criminal record. He filled out the application and sent it off. Sandra told him that he could be opening up a can of worms. He brushed that off proud that he was finally going to become a legal citizen. His rational was that once he got his citizenship no one would be able to deport him. Deportation had been a threat and intimidation tactic used against him many times over the past twenty years. When Drägo received the request for his presence at the immigration office, he left town taking a road trip five hundred miles east.

The police in that vicinity watched his every move, or so Randy the driver had told Sandra days before. Randy called her that morning wanting to know if she had heard from Drägo.

"Not a peep," Sandra told him.

He told her that the other department hadn't seen Drägo in three days at that point. Sandra got frustrated.

"Oh for crying out loud!" she exclaimed to Randy. "Do they not realize that he has probably left his car under their noses as a decoy? He usually rides the rails because he knows the police watch his car. Don't you guys know that? He could be anywhere by now!"

Randy felt foolish because none of the police including himself had ever thought about that scenario. It was a bleak thought reminding him of how elusive Drägo was.

"I'll find out if he's there or not myself," Sandra said disgusted.

"How are you going to do that?" Randy asked her, intrigued.

"I know the people he is staying with out there. I'll just phone there and ask for him. If he's not there they will tell me when he left and think nothing of it." Sandra said.

"Good plan!" Randy said, perking up again. "Let me know!"

"I will," Sandra told him.

She made the phone call. After a short casual conversation with the woman who answered the phone Sandra asked to speak with Drägo.

She was surprised when the woman said, "Sure, I'll get him. Hang on a minute."

Sandra really didn't expect him to be there because she had never known him to sit still for three days. He was surprised and happy to hear Sandra's voice. He told her he was leaving that day and would be home the next.

Sandra called Randy and said, "Ok, let's go. It's now or never. He's still where his car is, but he'll be back here tomorrow."

"Ok, good job Sandra," the police officer said to her. "We'll pick you up in about forty five minutes."

Sandra was brought back to the terrifying reality of the task at hand by Randy's voice. He was asking her for more specifics of the location. The party of three was close to its destination.

She was afraid for her life. She was afraid for her children. She was just plain afraid of everything all of a sudden. Fear had never been one of her weak points. It could be that maybe she just didn't know when to really be afraid. As in high thresholds of pain, she seemed to have a high threshold for fear. She often found herself commenting that there is a fine line between bravery and stupidity. Was this one of those instances? Sandra's mission was something that people only seen in movies. Was she making a massive mistake? It was too late to unring the bell. The sound of the engine purred in her ears as the car was maneuvered closer to the destination.

"It's right by that fence post," she told the officers.

They had reached their destination. The prized parcel they were looking for was quite likely buried in the snow. Weeks before city crews were trying to spend their snow-clearing budget for the year and had made wide highways out of what usually remained little more than cow paths during the winter. A ten-foot snow bank had buried the parcel making it impossible for Drägo, who had stashed it there, to find it.

The woman in the rear seat of the vehicle recalled previous excursions for the parcel. Usually the felon who did such things as bury parcels in the snow only went for the goods under the cover of darkness. Sandra had been elected several times to drive him to the hiding spot and wait at a coffee shop a few miles away while he frantically dug for his lost treasure in the ten foot snow bank. Sandra was never allowed to stop the vehicle if there were headlights anywhere within eyesight. In fact she was instructed to take a route completely away from the parcel if headlights appeared from any direction. When there were no headlights anywhere in sight Drägo deemed it safe to go to the site. Sandra was shooed away immediately as Drägo nearly jumped from her car with shovel in hand.

In total desperation, Drägo drove himself to the site in broad daylight after many unsuccessful attempts to find his parcel in the dark. Before panic set in he never wanted a car anywhere in the vicinity never mind in the daylight hours.

Sandra remembered February second of that year vividly, about six weeks earlier. A heavy fog draped the city. The temperature could have been considered balmy for that time of year. That was the first day the felon had done any digging in the daylight so the joke was that he was playing groundhog. The excavation site was on a road that was bordered on both sides by farmland located within two miles of the city's edge. A vehicle parked at the edge of the road in the middle of farmland would have looked suspicious or at the least, abandoned. A farmer or hiker might have reported it, seen enough times. That scenario was usually avoided at all cost. It was just too risky. It was also too costly not to find the parcel.

Drägo didn't find what he was looking for. He didn't find a lot of humor in the groundhog jokes either. In fact he was very agitated. He told Sandra that when he was leaving the site, he met a city police car on the road. Someone had reported him being there. It wasn't an area that would have had any patrol cars in it unless summoned. Drägo said if he had been there another five minutes he would have been caught digging. He suspected constant surveillance by the police and he was right in doing so. Randy told Sandra the first day they met that he had been assigned the job of trailing Drägo since the day he was released from prison. That had been normal procedure the last few times he was released.

Sandra wondered, *where was Randy on Groundhog Day and the several times previous when she had driven Drägo to the site*?

The police spent years and hundreds of thousands of dollars trying to stop the one-man crime-spree that always ensued upon Drägo's release. The organization often asks for help from civilians in their investigations. Hence, Crime Stoppers was formed. Sandra was the only person who could help them because she knew Drägo very well. Somebody had to help bring his career to a halt by beating him at his own game. The law desperately needed Sandra's help. She thought they could help each other in their common goal.

The unmarked police car arrived at the scene. A fence post marked the spot. The trouble was there was many fence posts. Sandra had to spot the right one.

"Are you able to get out of the car and show us exactly where it is?" Bill asked.

"Yes, I can get out of the car, but I won't," she told him. "Whose footprints would be more obvious than mine with two canes poking along beside?"

"Oh, ya, I guess you're right," came in response.

No guff, she kept to herself.

Sandra stayed in the back seat while both officers got out and went to the general area she had pointed out to them. There was no way she was leaving her footprints in the snow at that crime scene. She would be the next parcel buried.

No one went to the trunk of the car to pull out a shovel. Sandra had never been there before without seeing a shovel.

What kind of expedition is this? She wondered. *First there is no camera. Now there is no shovel. Isn't this ridiculous? How stupid can they be?*

It wasn't as if they didn't know the situation full well when she had agreed over the telephone just an hour before to go on the deadly mission. Sandra sat in the car in stealth mode. Her eyes darted in every direction. She was terrified that somehow Drägo would appear and see her with the police. She watched with mounting fear for her life as the officers kicked a little bit of snow around with their boots.

Yah, that ought a do it. Good job, boys! Kick around a few more flakes and let's get the hell out of here! Sandra's sarcastic side reared its ugly head.

The police didn't find what they were looking for either, but they did see traces of previous shovel digging. They came back to the car looking downhearted. The engine started again. The vehicle moved forward and then back again and stopped. Mumbling and more cop lingo came from the front seat.

Now what, Sandra thought, *more of the rubber boot shuffle?*

Finally there was something audible.

"I'm going to look further back that way," Randy indicated to Bill with a backward nod of his head.

"Ok. I'll stay here," his partner responded with a hint of a pout.

Randy got out of the car and walked down the snow packed road away from the rear of the car. Deep in their own thoughts Bill and Sandra had little to say to each other while they waited for Randy to come back. Sandra felt Bill's disappointment. She also felt her own emotions perking inside coming to a rapid boil. Relief, stupidity, disappointment and many more she couldn't distinguish all seemed to be fighting for attention. She just wanted to go home.

All of a sudden the driver's door flew open.

"I found it! It's just like she said it is, done up in bundles! I can even feel the elastic bands through the thickness of the two garbage bags!" Randy was very excited.

Bill flew out of the car and both officers ran to the parcel. Randy couldn't grab it, as he would have liked to. He went to get Bill because legally he couldn't touch the parcel without his partner as a witness.

Sandra couldn't even bring herself to watch them. She opened her car door and gagged up nothing.

"Oh my gawd, what have I done?" Sandra said aloud, throwing her head into her hands.

No one heard her. She knew that no one would care about her feelings because she had just lead the police officers to one of the biggest prizes of their careers. The police officers were ecstatic. Sandra's stomach churned. When she expressed her fear to the officers she sensed they really didn't want to hear about it. It was as if they were not going to allow her to burst their bubble or rain on their parade. Bill made a feeble attempt to console her by telling her that "yes" they should have brought a camera. It would have been a great snap shot for show and tell in a court room with the top one third of the plastic garbage bag sticking out of the snow after the big melt down. And "yes" she had done the right thing. Hell, she knew that already. She knew right from wrong. That's part of what drove her to risk her life and do what she did.

"That was pretty stupid of him to leave that just laying at the side of a road like that," Bill said after the car was moving again.

"Not really when you think about it." Sandra said. "When was the last time you checked out a garbage bag that you seen laying in a ditch or at the side of a road? Drägo often leaves parcels where no one would even give them a second glance, right out in the open."

"Good point, Sandra. I don't think I will ever be able to go by another garbage bag in my life without giving it a kick," Bill declared with a half-assed chuckle.

"Personally, I would have been more worried about some dog picking it up and taking it home, dropping it on his master's doorstep," Sandra commented.

"Yes, now that you mention it, that could have happened. Boy, I could sure use a dog like that!" Bill chuckled.

"So, how do you guys plan on explaining how you were able to find this prize?" Sandra asked warily.

"Guess we haven't thought about that yet," one of them said.

I was afraid of that, Sandra worried.

"Then let me tell you how you're going to explain it," she said.

She told them about Groundhog Day and that Drägo had met a city police car on the road as he was leaving the area. The obvious story would be that someone had reported him there so the investigating police force went on a digging expedition of their own to see what was so important to Drägo. The story stuck. Sandra was concerned that she was the one who had to come up with the explanation that would be told to Drägo. Could she dare leave the police to their own resources? She had visions of them telling Drägo that they watched him digging from some surveillance point. He would have known that wasn't true unless they were operating with telescopes from space.

Sandra could see that Drägo had strategically chosen the area for its many attributes. One very important one being there was nowhere for anyone to hide unless they somehow managed to conceal themselves behind a few six inch diameter trees. The location wasn't far from the city yet there were no houses within sight. The road was perfectly straight as far as roads go and it was the only one in the area. There were no roads connecting to it accept at each end. Anyone traveling through the area had no choice but to travel on that road because of the farmland it divided. The list of reasons for Drägo choosing that particular site seemed to go on forever in Sandra's mind.

Randy wasn't saying much of anything although he did acknowledge her story about Groundghog Day. He was in deep thought. When he did start talking it was a lot of mumbling in cop lingo again. Sandra got annoyed.

Damn it, she thought, *don't yap as if I'm not here. You wouldn't be here at all if it weren't for me.*

"What are you guys talking about?" she asked impatiently.

"We have to get to a phone to call our supervisor to tell him we have it," Randy said.

"Why don't you just use your radio?" she asked, making no effort to hide her annoyance.

"Because we have learned over the years when dealing with Drägo that we can't use our police radios. We don't trust him with cell phones either. I have to find a land line," he told her.

Sandra directed Randy to a small strip mall just inside the city where he was able to find a telephone. She was glad to hear the law had caught onto the radio thing. Years earlier during a rural undercover operation one of the police officers had told Sandra that Drägo always seemed to know where they were going to be sometimes even before they knew themselves. It was very frustrating for them. They asked Sandra at that time if she knew if he was into radios and the like. She told them he had taken a course in prison on radio and television repair.

By taking the police to the parcel, Sandra had orchestrated the ultimate betrayal and cardinal sin amongst the criminal population, particularly of her son's father, Drägo. The betrayal wasn't done out of spite for him. Some may call one of the reasons, "tough love." It was done so she and her two adult children could regain control of their own lives and because they couldn't morally live with Drägo's chosen profession.

As Randy was getting out of the car at the mall to find a landline he turned to Bill and said, "Don't leave town."

"I won't," Bill chuckled.

Chapter Two

Seventy five thousand dollars was sitting on the floor of the car between Bill's feet. While Sandra and Bill waited for Randy there wasn't much said between them. Randy came back to the car a few minutes later looking satisfied. Bill asked if their supervisor was as thrilled as they were. Randy assured him that the supervisor was. Sandra had seen that there was no pay phone on the mall parking lot. She asked Randy where he found a phone. He told her he used one at a dry cleaner's.

"How did you do that without somebody asking questions?" Sandra asked naively.

"I flashed my badge at him and told him I needed to use his phone. The man knows better than to ask questions when a badge is flashed in his face." Randy answered.

"Oh," Sandra said.

"Where's that other spot you are going to take us to?" Randy asked her.

"It's on Anderson Road," she said.

Randy drove the car in the direction of the road. They would be there in about fifteen minutes. Randy and Bill starting talking between themselves again. Sandra didn't care what they were saying anymore. Her mind wandered off recalling the past twenty-two years and the events that lead up to her betrayal of Drägo. He had been in and out of prison since Sandra had met him when she was seventeen years old. Drägo was twenty years old and freshly out of a penitentiary.

"As long as he is on parole, Mom, so are we," was a statement her daughter Susan had made before the money had ever entered the picture.

No truer words were ever spoken in that case. Sandra repeated that comment to Bill one day. His response made Sandra even more determined to get the man out of her family's life.

"Yes, Sandra that is true, even more so than you realize," Bill's voice faded off as he spoke the last part of the sentence, as if in deep thought.

He wasn't about to tell her anymore, but Sandra realized the enormity of what he had said. He knew she would pick up on it and that he had said all that was necessary. She was also testing him to clarify the reality of the situation. She had a good handle on what was going on.

Whenever Drägo had been released from prison he hunted for Sandra and her children if he didn't know where they were. His hunt for them was only to be near them in an attempt to be a family in his own odd way. The law never had to hunt far for the family. All they had to do was follow Drägo, which was always one of their top priorities anyway. The law was always informed of the exact date of his prison release that over the years came no sooner than mandatory parole.

Sandra and her adult children had no lives whenever Drägo was on the street. Where they went and whom they associated with became well known amongst the investigating team and their superiors. The cops even went so far as to follow Sandra to her physiotherapy appointments. She was in a wheel chair before and after her joint replacements. She went to physio three times a week. Sandra wondered if the police expected the physiotherapist's table might be a rendezvous point.

My goodness, she thought when she first saw one them looking right at her appearing to be holding up a wall at the hospital.

I'm not the one you should be watching so closely, damn it, she wanted to shout at him.

She glared at him instead. Their eyes locked on each other's for a few seconds.

What the hell do you think is going to happen here? Where is the guy you are really looking for? Sandra thought.

As much as Sandra always spoke straight to the point sometimes she just kept the point to herself. She had learned when and when not to speak.

Cripes, I can't even be sick, Sandra drawled to herself. *My life is a mess.*

Twenty minutes after she got home from physio that day Sandra was startled by someone hammering on her apartment door. It had to be either the Mafia or the law with that violent knocking. Sandra wasn't expecting the Mafia. She had been lying on the couch and was dosing off. Physio had a tendency to exhaust her. She couldn't walk without hanging onto something, a protruding edge of a wall, a counter, or furniture. Her wheelchair was left dripping on a long runner mat at the door when she went into the apartment because of sloppy conditions outside.

The knocking became more persistent. A male voice shouted her name.

She yelled, "Who is it?"

There was no answer. At first she stayed near the phone in the living room. She was sure she already knew who it was, but had to be cautious because she could barely stand on her own two feet. She couldn't let just anyone in. She was alone. She finally did make her way to the door. Before Sandra got it open the man shouted again asking if she was looking through the peephole. She gave him the same courtesy he had given her and didn't answer him. She opened the door to find two very tall men standing there looking as if they were full of authority. Sandra knew they had to be plain clothed police officers. She could almost pick a cop out of a crowd by that point in her life.

"I'm too short to be looking through the peep hole," she stated the obvious.

Sandra was less than five feet tall. Mostly little girls looked at her not quite sure what to make of her. Sandra remembers being in a store with a friend of hers and telling a story of how little girls often reacted to her. They would timidly sidle up beside her to see if Sandra was taller than they were. Most were not far from her height. Sandra was no sooner done telling the cute story when two little girls started whispering between themselves and looking at Sandra. As if on a dare one of the girls did exactly what Sandra had just finished describing.

Sandra stood still allowing herself to be compared with the girl's height. Sandra remembers being in a store once and meeting a little boy with his grandmother. The little boy kept watching Sandra. She saw him and smiled.

The boy turned to his grandmother and asked, "Is that a lady, Grama?"

One of the police officers almost burst out laughing with Sandra's reference to her height. The other stood there looking down at her oblivious to the humor in the scene. It was Randy.

Sandra knew why they were there. They came to pick her brain. It wasn't the first time over the years that the police had come to her hoping for information. She watched them slop half way across her kitchen floor leaving huge muddy footprints. There was no thought to remove their footwear. They just tramped in. Sandra wasn't impressed.

"I can't clean that mess up," she told them looking down at the floor and then up at them.

She had just stated the obvious again. They could see that she could barely walk. Both of them stopped in their sloppy tracks and looked down at their feet.

"Oh ya, I guess we should have taken our shoes off," Dick, the guy with the sense of humor, said to Randy.

"Yes, you should have. After you do that you will find a rag under the sink that you can wipe your mess up with," Sandra said obviously pissed off.

Their authoritarian demeanor disappeared. Like kids who had just been disciplined they went back to the doormat and removed their shoes. Dick reached into the cupboard under the kitchen sink and found the rag that Sandra had mentioned. He wiped the floor with it. Randy remained oblivious.

Sandra invited them to have a seat at the kitchen table. There wasn't anything of any real importance said that day. Sandra felt she had to get a good handle on the situation before she could be comfortable telling them anything. She wanted to stop Drägo as much as they did, but she was afraid. She told them flat out that Drägo could come to the door at any time. That information didn't seem to faze them. Sandra thought after that maybe they knew something she didn't, as in where Drägo was at that time. At least she hoped that was the case.

Both officers asked her some questions about Drägo's habits. She answered as best as she cared to. Dick wasn't from the local jurisdiction. When Sandra asked why he was involved, he said Drägo had spent a considerable amount of time within his jurisdiction that was a three-hour drive away. He also said that he had a particular interest in the case because years earlier when Drägo had escaped from a penitentiary he was the officer assigned to bring him back to the gated community. Sandra knew the incident Dick was talking about. Drägo was on the lam for three months. He didn't know where Sandra and the kids were at the time and couldn't risk contact with them anyway. Dick said it was one of the most interesting cases he had ever worked on.

Sandra thought, *ya, I'll bet it was.*

Randy was from the local headquarters. He told Sandra that they had both been on the police force for about thirteen years. In their entire careers they never failed to hear Drägo's name. Randy was heading up the investigation. She thought he had the personality of a stick. She knew this was serious business and not a personality contest, but she could see that Randy worked strictly by the book. Not being a conventional type person she didn't care for that kind of approach. Randy hedged a lot whenever he spoke about Drägo as well, so Sandra felt like even though he had come to her for help he wouldn't trust her. Mistrust seemed to be running rampant. Yet Dick spoke openly to her. She remained civil to Randy, but she knew he wasn't someone she would be able to work with although she did admit to him that there was a lot more to be said. She let it be known that she didn't feel comfortable talking to them. Should it ever be discovered that she had been talking to them about anything incriminating she would be killed. She told them so. They didn't doubt her. They said they didn't want to put her in any danger. Sandra pointed out that just their presence in her apartment could put her in danger.

Before the detectives left Sandra's apartment, Dick wandered into the living room. He spotted a picture of her daughter Susan who was twenty-one years old.

"Is this your daughter?" he asked Sandra, looking at the picture.

"Yes, it is." Sandra answered.

"I guess she's married with a family," Dick said as more of a question than a statement.

"No she isn't. She lives here with her mother. So back off!" she glared at him.

"Whoa, Mom!" he said, looking surprised raising his hands in defense. "I didn't mean to upset you, but your daughter is a very beautiful girl."

The stick personality laughed then and said to his partner, "Well, I guess you can consider yourself told."

Sandra almost felt bad about the way she had instantly jumped on the guy. She smiled at him after Randy's comment. The two police officers left. Two or three weeks would pass before she would have contact with either one of them again.

In the meantime Sandra kept her eyes and ears wide open whenever Drägo was around. He was at her apartment daily, sometimes twice a day. He started giving her more detail when she nibbled around the edges of conversations asking questions. He thought she had finally become interested in his career and didn't see it as distasteful anymore. Sandra was pretending that she had given up fighting him on it.

Drägo told her everything. He laughed when he told her about the police following him one night after he had pulled off a job. He said it was snowing like hell that particular night. He shut his headlights off and turned off the highway onto a gravel road. Drägo said he couldn't see anything. He was driving very slowly just feeling the road underneath his car. The unmarked police car carried on down the highway. It appeared to the cops that the car they were following had dropped off the face of the earth. Drägo was very proud of himself when he relayed the event to Sandra.

Sandra absorbed everything and read between the lines when Drägo spoke in riddles. That was a habit of his. She couldn't be too persistent in her questioning. A sudden keen interest in Drägo's activities would have made him suspicious of her. She couldn't have that happen because from the moment she became involved in the investigation, she felt responsible for stopping him. The police had proven they couldn't do it alone. Drägo was relentless in his career. When on a mission, Sandra was relentless as well.

Within a week or two of the two officers visiting Sandra, she spoke to another officer on the phone that had worked undercover investigating Drägo several years earlier. She called him. She felt she could trust him because they had dealings before. He knew better than to upset her since he had done that once. That had caused him some grief.

He was surprised to hear from her and said, "Hey how the hell are you, Sandra? Long time no speak."

He wanted to know how she found him because he had been through many transfers within the force since they had met.

"Well, like the police I have my ways to," Sandra chuckled into the phone.

The two had a couple of easygoing, yet serious, conversations over the course of a week. He asked her to call Randy since he was the investigating officer in Drägo's case. Sandra agreed to call him but made no promise as to when. The same officer called her a few days later and asked her if she had called Randy. She said she hadn't, as if he didn't know that already. Sandra told him that if the guy really wanted to talk to her again he should call her. She didn't really want to talk to Randy but would if he made the next move. It was her way of letting the stick personality know that if she did get involved in the investigation he wasn't going to control her. She wanted to wait and see just how badly he did want to talk to her. It gave her a chance to test the waters.

Randy was eager to talk to her and had been hoping she would call. He called Sandra that same day. Questions and answers went back and forth between the pair daily by telephone. He asked questions. She mostly answered questions. That went on for a couple of weeks. Sandra still had the feeling that Randy mistrusted her even though she was spilling everything she knew, which was lots. He started questioning her about things they both knew the answers to as if he was trying to slip her up.

At one point a surveillance team had been set up at a specific address and time. Sandra had given Randy the time and place. It was in downtown Riverside, a large city. Randy phoned her just before the rendezvous time. Sandra heard panic in his voice. The team couldn't find the place they were looking for. Time was of the essence. She told Randy it was within a couple of blocks of Riverside City Police department headquarters and he should probably go there and ask for directions because she didn't know the downtown area well enough to direct him.

Randy questioned Sandra later on the phone with a tone she didn't like, "So, what happened there?"

Sandra was really frustrated with that and didn't try to hide it.

She came close to shouting at him when she said, "Well, you tell me! You were there! I wasn't!"

She was thinking, cripes, I give you people the information. Isn't it up to you to do something with it? Why get snotty with me because you damn near screwed up?

She didn't have to say it. Her tone of voice said it all.

Drägo had places to go where he didn't want to take his car. He knew the surveillance was heavy. He didn't say that but Sandra knew he was looking for a reprieve from it. He asked Susan to switch cars with him. She mentioned it to Sandra and said she didn't want to switch with him because she didn't want the police following her in his car. Her mother told her that once the police saw her in the car they wouldn't bother to follow her. As well, Susan didn't want her car found at some crime scene. Neither did Sandra. Sandra told her to make the switch and that she would inform the police of it. There was no good excuse for Susan not switching vehicles with Drägo that either mother or daughter could think of. Sandra didn't want to raise any suspicions on anyone's part. There was just no way to refuse. Sandra was in too deep with the police to not let them know what was happening. Randy would be furious with her if she didn't tell him. She couldn't have blamed him for that and didn't want to give him any excuse to ball her out either.

The switch took place in the parking lot where Susan worked, right on schedule. The police picked up on the trail of her car from there. Sandra still does not know why Randy spoke to her the way he did asking her what had happened there. Everything seemed cut and dried to her. She asked Susan if anything unusual had happened. Susan said nothing had happened. She had expressed concern to her mother before hand that she didn't know if she was going to be able to pull it off without suspiciously looking around to see where the police were. She didn't like the idea of knowing there was a surveillance team watching her meeting with Drägo.

Sandra sympathized but said to Susan, "It's not like it'll be the first time the police have watched you."

"I know, but its the first time that I'll be aware of them," Susan told her mother. "I just hate this, Mom!"

"I know, Susan. So do I, but this can't go on forever. We just have to keep persevering," the mother sympathized.

Sandra worried that her daughter might crumble under the pressure and blow the whistle on everyone thinking she would be doing all of them a favor, including Drägo.

Susan often said things like, "Mom, I'm sick of this. Why don't we just tell him what's going on already!"

The consequences of letting Drägo know what was going on hadn't occurred to Susan. It was an extremely tension filled time for the family.

Randy's panic to find the place made it evident to Sandra that he didn't want to let Drägo out of his sight for even a few minutes. He wanted to be right there when the switch was made so Drägo's trail didn't go cold. Randy needed time to set up the surveillance team before Drägo arrived. Sandra felt that Susan probably was followed in Drägo's car to make sure there wasn't anything-shady happening on the family's part. Sandra never told her that. Some things were better left unsaid.

On first telephone contact with Randy, Sandra was told that if he wasn't there at any point she could talk to his partner, Bill. She ended up talking with Bill several times in one week. They called each other daily. Sandra found him pleasant to talk to. He actually had a personality. Unlike his partner, Bill wasn't stuck on going by the book. It was a relief to Sandra, but finally she had to ask where Randy was.

"Randy is away on another case, but he'll be back next week," Bill told her.

"Hmm," was the only response he heard.

"What do you mean, hmm? Is there something wrong, Sandra?" Bill asked.

He noticed she was hesitant to speak. Bill knew her well enough by then to know that wasn't like her.

Choosing her words carefully she simply said, "Yes, there is."

"What is it, Sandra?" Bill's curiosity peaked.

She heard concern in his voice. She was still hesitant. Sandra didn't know how much she should say to Randy's partner about Randy. She did know that if she continued working with him everyone's case was going to fall apart. Hers and the police department's.

Sandra realized she couldn't keep the man on the other end of the telephone line in suspense any longer so she set her hesitation aside and ventured, "I don't think Randy trusts me."

"Why do you say that, Sandra?" Bill asked very concerned and surprised.

"Because he questions me like he's trying to trick me or something, as if he's trying to catch me in a lie. He seems to dance around the obvious a lot and it makes me wonder why. He was also quite indignant one morning when I didn't get to the phone in time. He asked where I was in a snotty tone that I have heard too much of. Contrary to popular belief lately I do have a life. My sole purpose in life is not to be sitting by the phone waiting for Randy to call," she told him.

Bill sounded sympathetic when he said, "Well, I'm sorry to hear all of this, Sandra. Trying to apprehend Drägo can be very taxing on us and we can tend to get a little anxious at times. Randy was probably just having one of those anxious moments at that time when he couldn't get you on the phone. As for the trust part, I know from briefings we have that Randy is very happy with the information you have been giving us. He is a good cop and is very good at what he does."

"I don't doubt for a second that he is very good at his job. I guess we'll have to chalk it up to a personality conflict or whatever, but I really don't like working with the guy," Sandra told him.

She felt she was sticking her neck out risking everything she had worked so hard toward. She had to do it. After weeks of working with Randy daily, Sandra just couldn't change her opinion. She plainly didn't like him and felt that he didn't like her either. She was doing absolutely everything in her power to help him, yet he still treated her like she wasn't to be trusted. Sandra wasn't happy, but she did recall an incident that happened years earlier when the police felt betrayed by her. The officer who asked her to call Randy would have told him about it.

"The last thing we want is for you to be unhappy, Sandra. We really appreciate your help. You've worked with me while Randy has been away. Do you have any concerns where our working relationship is concerned?" Bill asked her.

"No, I don't. You don't have that by the book attitude of Randy's. I don't operate by the book. You haven't made me think that you don't trust me either," Sandra said. "I don't know what we're going to do about this, but I do know that I don't want to talk to Randy anymore."

"Well, again, I'm sorry to hear this, Sandra, but I can fix it for you. You don't have to do anything that you don't want to do. And you don't have to talk to anyone you don't want to talk to. You know that I will have to mention this to my supervisor though, so we can straighten this out," Bill told her.

"Yes, I know. You do whatever you have to do. Just fix this situation before we all lose out here," she said.

"I will." Bill vowed.

Sandra never spoke with Randy again. She recalled the first time she had actually called him. It was nighttime. Drägo was skulking around her apartment in peak stealth mode. He said he had to leave right away after being there for about fifteen minutes. Sandra wondered why he had bothered to come at all since he was in such a hurry to leave. She realized that Drägo's visit to her apartment was nothing more than a ruse. He was very nervous. That made Sandra nervous. She thought she had better call Randy. Something was up and she wanted to make sure the police were on the trail.

"Something is going to happen tonight," she told Randy after Drägo left.

"Do you know where something is going to happen?" Randy asked.

"No, but I can guarantee you that it won't be in Riverside," Sandra said.

"What makes you so sure it won't happen in the city?" Randy asked her.

"Because Drägo only hits small towns," she said.

"Do you know why he only hits small towns?" he asked curiously.

"No, I don't know the reasoning behind it. I just know that it's a fact," she said. "I'm just calling to make sure you're on him because tonight is definitely the night."

"Thanks, Sandra. We'll be on him," Randy said.

Randy's partner, Bill took over the informant part of the investigation after a discussion with the team's supervisor. Sandra felt bad for Randy to have to be told that she would not work with him anymore. She had to do what she was comfortable with for everyone's sake, including Randy's. He was still the headman in the investigation and wanted Drägo off the street as much as anyone did. It would go better for him if Sandra dealt with someone else. In the weeks to follow, Bill and Sandra made several calls a day back and forth to each other. Communications improved immensely.

One evening, Drägo showed up unexpected at Sandra's apartment and asked her to go for a drive with him. There wasn't anything unusual about that because they often went out for coffee, lunch or anywhere at all really. That time Drägo hadn't said where they were going. That was unusual. When Sandra asked he wouldn't tell her.

"Just come with me," he said mysteriously.

Sandra was wary, but didn't dare show it because showing signs of fear could be a deadly mistake for her. Since the outing was unexpected she didn't have a chance to call Bill telling him about the potentially dangerous situation. She saw Drägo's rational in showing up unexpected. He usually called her first. That time he didn't want to chance a telephone conversation being monitored. Knowing Drägo's reasoning, Sandra's fear increased. Both her and the police lived with the fact that Drägo could catch onto what she was doing at any time. There were times when Bill thought that Drägo may be setting Sandra up to confirm any suspicions he may have had about her involvement in the investigation. Bill's supervisor told him to mention the possibility of the Witness Protection Program to Sandra. He asked where Sandra might want to go if it ever came to that. Sandra hoped it would not happen, but preliminary plans were made just in case.

Drägo was in top stealth mode when he picked up Sandra. He was acting nervous like he did before he went out to do a job. During their trip, he constantly watched in his rear view mirror for headlights to see if anyone was following him. That wasn't unusual. He always drove like that day or night. As Randy had said, Drägo never drove in a straight line at any time. He would zigzag across the city hoping to evade any would be surveillance. Sandra knew that he always put on many miles more than necessary getting from point A to B. She had driven with him many times. That unusual driving habit annoyed Sandra and the police. That night it frightened her, prolonging her anxiety about where he was taking her. Drägo was making a particularly special effort to make sure that no one was following him by driving around the city longer than he normally would have.

After zigzagging around the city, Drägo turned onto a gravel road leaving the lights of the city behind them. He still wouldn't tell Sandra where they were going. All he would say was that he didn't want to talk about it. She was horrified, but couldn't let him know that. She worried that Drägo might be able to hear her heart. In the grip of fear it seemed to be ready to pop out of her chest. It pounded in her ears.

It was a cloudy overcast night. Sandra couldn't even see any stars. She watched the road that was only illuminated by the car's headlights. The tension was as thick as the darkness that veiled each side of the road.

Drägo steered the vehicle down the road making a couple of turns onto more gravel roads. He was almost crouched behind the steering wheel constantly watching for other signs of life. There were none. The road came to a dead end. Drägo stopped the car in the completely deserted area where even lights from houses didn't come into view. He turned off the only visible headlights, his own. He told Sandra to get out of the car. She tried to beg off by complaining about how difficult it was for her to do that because she could hardly walk or stand. Drägo insisted. Sandra got out of the car. When her eyes adjusted to the darkness she saw that they were parked beside a heavily wooded area. The site he had taken her to would be the perfect place to leave a body. No one would see or hear anything. It could be a dead end for Sandra as well. Sandra resigned herself to the fact that she was going to die there. She didn't fear the dying part. She feared the slow calculated beating that would be the cause.

Sandra thought, *this is it. The gig's up. He's known all along what I have been doing. I'm surprised he didn't kill me before this. I guess he was just waiting to make sure, to have enough proof, before he murdered his son's mother. I wonder if there was one particular incident that tipped him off. Where did I go wrong*?

Drägo arrived at the passenger side of the car where she had got out. Sandra had left the car door open as if it would provide an escape for her. Drägo closed it. He stood beside her.

Sandra stood on her wobbly legs waiting for him to make his move on her when he asked in hushed tones, "See that tree right there?"

"Which one?" she gulped back fear.

Drägo pointed. "That one right there with the fork in that big branch."

"Oh, ya, ok." Sandra said, squinting to see.

She was leery of the reason for him pointing out one particular tree among the many. Was he going to tell her next to take a real good look at it because the next time she would see it would be from the ground up? Was he going to bury her under it? She was petrified.

"Remember that tree if I should get picked up or anything stupid like that," he told her. "There will be money buried under it."

Ok, she thought. Her voice sounded shaky, "But why did I have to get out of the car for you to show me that?"

In the same breath she dared to ask, "And where the hell are we anyway?"

Sandra knew she would never find the place again. She needed an identifiable location, like a name.

"We're on Anderson Road. You had to get out of the car because we never know if the car is bugged or not," Drägo told her. "I don't like talking about anything like this inside the car. You know that."

Sandra did know that. It hadn't occurred to her in her fear. She was sure her phony knees would collapse into a pile of titanium rubble. Drägo helped Sandra get back into the car. He took her home with little zigzagging of the city and then went home himself. Sandra nearly fell into her bed when she got home. She was very weak. Her whole body was shaking as if in aftershock.

Sandra still hadn't quite recovered from the terrifying experience when Bill called her early the next morning. She told him all about it.

"Why did you go with him?" Bill asked her in surprise.

"Because I had no choice. I couldn't refuse because that alone would have made him suspicious of me. I go out with him lots of times. You know that!" Sandra said incredulously.

She thought, *was that a stupid question with an obvious answer*?

"Weren't you scared?" Bill asked making no effort to conceal his fear for her.

"Of course! I was scared absolutely shitless! I thought I was done for," she told him.

"Well, I guess so!" he said. "Thank God it wasn't what it looked like. You have to be careful of him, Sandra. Your life really is at risk."

"You don't need to tell me that. I know that better than anyone does. There was no time to call you to give you a heads up," she said.

Then she thought, *and where the hell was everybody anyway when I was out there risking my neck*?

"Just be very careful, Sandra," Bill warned with an ominous tone in his voice.

"I'm trying," she told him. "But what the hell could I do?"

Sandra heard concern in Bill's voice and knew it was genuine. Since she had started working solely with him, she had telephone numbers where he could be reached day or night, on or off shift, including his home phone number. The situation they were dealing with was heating up. Both Sandra and Bill surmised that was because Drägo thought that Sandra didn't stand as an obstacle to him anymore. He wasn't trying to hide what he was doing so he became even more sure of himself than he already had been, if that was possible.

Another evening not long after that Drägo called Sandra and asked her if the kids were home. She said they were not and asked why he wanted to know.

"I'm coming over," he said and hung up the phone.

Sandra got scared and called Bill. They both worried about what could be on Drägo's mind that time. There was nothing that either one of them could do but wait. Sandra knew the surveillance team would follow Drägo to her apartment building and sit outside but that was as good as it would get. She waited and worried.

Drägo was there in about ten minutes. He looked nervous, but there was something different about his nervousness that night. It really frightened Sandra, but again, she couldn't let him know that.

They had some idle chatter for quite a while before Drägo asked her a question.

"If I was to straighten out my life, would you marry me?" he asked sincerely.

Sandra started to laugh. If she hadn't laughed she would have surely cried.

"You, straighten out! You damn pretzel, you," she said to Drägo trying to make a joke of it.

"Ya, I guess you're right. That will never happen," he said, laughing, but looked surprised and disappointed at the same time.

Sandra felt bad for him. They talked a while longer before Drägo left. Sandra's phone rang within seconds of Drägo closing her apartment door. When she answered it she heard Bill's voice.

"What the hell are you doing calling me right now?" she whispered into the phone, "Drägo just left. He could be standing right outside the door yet."

Bill said he didn't know exactly where Drägo was, but the team was still outside her building.

Sandra thought, *Whoop Dee Do* and almost hung up the phone before Bill said Drägo had just walked out the front door of her building.

She thought his call was very risky, but realized he called to find out if she was dead or alive. An hour or more had passed since Drägo had arrived at her apartment. Sandra knew that Bill would be getting very agitated outside.

"What did he want?" Bill asked anxiously.

"He wants to get married," Sandra told him.

"Married? To who?" he asked sounding incredulous.

"To me for gawd sake! Who do you think?" she asked him just as incredulously.

"What did you say?" Bill asked stunned.

"I said no," Sandra told him.

Bill was flabbergasted. Sandra was flabbergasted as well, but only because Bill was flabbergasted. He came to her apartment the next morning.

"I'm sure glad you didn't take Drägo up on his proposal," he said to Sandra, sounding overly relieved.

"That would be pretty stupid of me. Wouldn't it?" she said.

"Well, it would certainly be your choice, Sandra, but I don't think it would be a wise one," Bill said to her. "Do you think there would ever be a chance that he might straighten out?"

"No," she said without hesitation.

Sandra felt like Bill had come to check up on her. Was he concerned he might lose his only ace in the case? A wedding would have put a completely different slant on everything. In fact, the case could have quickly gone to hell in a hand basket. Bill mentioned during a phone conversation before then that there seemed to be some kind of a magnet to Riverside for Drägo. He said he couldn't figure it out and asked Sandra if she knew what it might be. Sandra pointed out that his son lived there. Bill said he thought there was more to it than that. Sandra didn't bite. She didn't appreciate the way Bill tried to make everything in her life his business. She felt that constant surveillance and more than likely a telephone tap had put enough of a damper on her personal life. What personal life? She didn't have one.

One thing she purposely made Bill's business was a planned trip with Drägo. Sandra called Bill to tell him that Drägo and her were going on a trip some fifteen hundred miles away. Drägo had asked her to go to his mother's with him. She tried talking her way out of it, but couldn't. Drägo looked at her oddly when she kept persisting that she shouldn't go. There was really no good excuse as to why she couldn't go because her physiotherapy sessions were finished and she was retired on disability.

"So are you telling me that the team can take a rest?" Bill asked, sounding happy for any reprieve.

"Yes, I guess that's what I'm telling you. So I guess that means you won't be making the trip," Sandra chuckled. "Do you anticipate any other surveillance on us while we're away?"

"No, I don't, Sandra. Have a good trip," Bill said. "Let me know when you get back, so I'll know when the team has to rally together again."

Drägo and Sandra made the trip arriving at his mother's unscathed by the winter road conditions. It was in February soon after Groundhog Day. His mother was happy to see them both. She had always wished they would get married. That might mean that her son would end his career. It was wishful thinking on a mother's part. Sandra always felt sorry for Drägo's mother in that regard, but having a family hadn't stopped Drägo before. What would have changed?

Drägo was upset by the fact that his mother wouldn't let Sandra and him sleep together in her house. Sandra thought it was funny and had expected that. She couldn't believe that Drägo was surprised by it. She thought maybe she should have mentioned it to him before they got there. Sandra and Drägo's mother had always got along well, like friends, whether Drägo was in the picture or not.

Susan called her mother the following day. She wanted to join them. She arrived the next day at the international airport.

Sandra woke up in the middle of the night to find Drägo standing beside the bed she was sleeping on in his mother's house. He was dressed as if he had been outside, coat and all. Seeing that he had startled her he motioned for her to be quiet. He showed her a wad of cash. It was four thirty in the morning and Drägo felt the need to boast. She looked at him and shook her head in scorn and disbelief that he would do such a thing from his mother's house. She thought she might find herself driving back to Riverside alone because Drägo could be arrested if he didn't smarten up. She wasn't happy.

Susan and Sandra had a small trip planned for that same day. Drägo would not be joining them. He stayed behind to spend time alone with his mother. Mother and daughter left in the car.

The two women went to visit an uncle of Sandra's. From there they went to see Susan's father who lived thirty miles away. Susan was twenty-one years old. She had never met her father, but decided it might be time she did.

Since they lived with a considerable distance between them and the rest of the family, it wasn't difficult to keep Susan's father's real identity from her until Sandra felt she was old enough to have a chance at coping with his personality disorders more than she could have as a small child. Susan knew that Drägo wasn't her father, but never questioned her mother about it. She was fourteen before her mother made her biological father's whereabouts known to her. It was Susan's choice as to whether or not she contacted him. Susan spoke with her father a few times over the telephone only to decide that he really wasn't someone she wanted to meet. Sandra never said anything about the man except that he couldn't hold a job. She left it up to Susan to form her own opinions. Susan had contact with her uncle and his family as well, and secretly kept that, feeling the need for some kind of rapport with that side of her family.

Sandra thought her fourteen years of silence regarding her daughter's true identity might seem unfair. She resented being hidden from her own mother when she was a child. But what would have been unfair would have been to expect a small child to be able deal with a person who adults found extremely difficult to deal with. He lived in a bubble of chronic paranoia bordering on insanity. If Sandra were a professional opining on the subject, she would probably refer to it as exactly that, insanity. Should that bubble ever burst, she believed an institution would become his home. He lived under psychiatric care and was on medications at all times.

Susan had inherited some of her father's paranoid traits. Sandra's brother mentioned it when Susan was ten years old. Sandra had already seen it. Her brother mentioned it because he didn't know if Sandra was aware of the personality traits he saw in his niece. Sandra had

Susan receive some counseling because of it. She knew that if Susan had been raised under her father's influence the child would have been much worse off than she was. Once she got married, things improved in that way because her husband, Luke, pointed out the same things to Susan that Sandra had been telling her all of her life. Oddly enough, Luke and Susan had met just before Susan met her father. There are no accidents.

When the women left the father's home they were barely outside when Susan turned to her mother and said, "My gawd, Mom! Is he ever paranoid!"

"Yes! Isn't that something? Now you know why I have been concerned about your paranoia all of your life." Sandra said to her.

"Well, yes, but he is ridiculous! I have never seen anyone as paranoid as he is," Susan said.

The two women got in their car getting back on the highway relieved to be away from Susan's father. They had a two-hour drive ahead of them to their destination of a major city.

Chapter Three

Sandra thought back to the time in her life when she got married. Hubby was nineteen. She was sixteen. The marriage lasted a disastrous six months. Hubby had seven jobs in that time. Sandra worked full time in a restaurant barely making enough to feed and house them. She was two months pregnant with Susan when she left her husband.

Her child's grown up voice brought her back to the present. They were getting close to the bustling metropolis they were destined for.

"Mom, let me drive, so I can say I drove in that massive city," Susan said, smiling.

"Sure, go for it," Sandra smiled as she prepared to pull onto the shoulder of the road.

Susan and Sandra arrived in the city at approximately midnight. Since they had missed a highway exit for a motel strip they ended up right in the downtown core of the city. They needed to find a room, but because they didn't have a clue as to where they were going they found themselves at the waterfront. Sandra said they better get out of there because it was known to be a bad area of the city. They didn't see a decent looking hotel anywhere. There were lots of seedy ones around, but they would have rather slept in the car than in one of those. Sandra suggested they go into a twenty-four hour coffee shop they had passed and ask a waitress or somebody that was familiar with the downtown area.

Susan drove around the block to get back to the coffee shop. She parked the car and both women went inside. They thought of safety in numbers. Sandra went directly to the washroom. She thought her bladder was going to burst. When she came out, Susan was talking to a cab driver seated at the counter. He was trying to explain directions to a decent hotel. The directions were complicated to Susan who didn't know the city. Susan and the driver went to his car so he could show her his city map. It was parked right outside the completely glassed front wall of the coffee shop, but Sandra went and stood outside and watched anyway making her presence known. The driver took notice of her. He left his door open showing Susan the map. Another taxi pulled up to the curb at the street. The driver tooted his horn at Sandra. She waved him on letting him know that she didn't need a taxi.

Susan came up to her then and said the taxi driver was going to lead them to a hotel. When they were traveling on the tail of the taxi, Susan asked why the other taxi driver had tooted his horn. Sandra explained that he was looking for a fare and hoped that she was it.

"Maybe he thought we were a pair of hookers, Mom." Susan said.

"I doubt that, Susan," Sandra said, smiling at her daughter.

"Ya never know, Mom!" Susan said.

When was the last time you seen a hooker on two canes?" Sandra asked.

"Oh ya, I guess not," Susan chuckled.

The women got into a hotel room and got ready for bed almost immediately. Susan wanted to see the view of the city lights from their high vantage point up several stories in the hotel. When she opened the drapes both women laughed. The only thing they could see was a solid brick wall of another building. Susan closed the drapes. They got into bed and went to sleep.

The mother and daughter got up the next morning and set out to do some exploring in the city. Susan pushed her mother out of the hotel in her wheelchair. Sandra couldn't walk any distance on her canes.

They went to two different locations of the Hard Rock Café. They expected more atmosphere than what they saw although one was at the top of a sky dome. Everyone always talked about the Hard Rock Café. Susan and Sandra couldn't see what the fuss was all about.

For lunch they went to a revolving restaurant that towered and crept above the skyline over the city. Both of them were astounded by the prices on the menu. They both had hamburger platters and an alcoholic beverage. The bill for lunch was eighty-five dollars. Sandra left a hundred dollar bill on the table. The view was terrific from the top of the tower. No doubt they had just paid lots to see it.

Around four thirty in the afternoon, Susan suggested they should leave the city and go back to Drägo's mothers. Sandra said they should wait until after rush hour. Two hours later Susan became impatient and said they should go. Sandra agreed, but warned Susan that the traffic would still be savage on the expressways in and out of the city.

Susan wanted to drive. She was astounded by the amount of traffic on the freeway. It was almost bumper-to-bumper traveling sixty miles an hour. Those were the slow drivers. Most were exceeding that speed. Susan had never seen anything like it, at least not that she remembered. Sandra told her she was doing fine, but not to stop at merge signs when she entered into the traffic flow or she would get rear ended because drivers behind her wouldn't expect her to stop. Susan had to literally go with the flow. The flow was extremely heavy and intense. An air horn sounded from a semi directly behind them. Sandra knew it would scare Susan.

"What did I do, Mom?" she asked, panicking.

"You didn't do anything. That semi driver blew his air horn at that little blue car right up there. I was watching in my mirror. It squeezed in between the semi and us taking off into that lane further over. Don't worry. You're doing just fine. Just keep on driving like you are, holding your own. I don't care how big that semi looks in your mirror. He's not there to intimidate you. He just wants to get out of this chaos the same as we do," Sandra said.

Susan relaxed after that and drove like a champion in the mayhem of traffic. She commented after they were out of the worst of it that she knew the traffic would be heavy, but she hadn't expected anything like what it was. She said it was a good thing they hadn't left at four thirty because it would have been much worse. There was a point when they had first entered onto the freeway that Susan suggested that maybe her mother should drive. Susan knew that Sandra had driven on that particular freeway many times. Sandra pointed out that there was no place to pull off the highway to be able to switch seats even if it was necessary. Besides Sandra thought it was a good driving experience for Susan. If she could drive on those freeways, she would be able to drive anywhere. Sandra knew rural women who drove to the edge of Riverside and parked their cars. Then they took a city bus wherever they wanted to go.

A few years later, Steve had the same driving experience with his mother at eleven o'clock at night. The traffic was insane even at that late hour. He couldn't believe it either, but drove like a champion as well. Sandra remembered her first time behind the wheel on the same freeways.

The children were babies at the time. Drägo had to go to court in the same vicinity. He told Sandra he didn't want her to be there in case something dire happened, as in him being sentenced to jail. He didn't want her to see that. Sandra disregarded what he had said and took the kids to her aunt's for the day. Then she headed out onto the highway in her car. She needed to know what was happening. The outcome concerned her family's future.

Sandra got lost. She drove right past the freeway exit that would take her to the presiding courtroom. She drove for a long time because there was no way out unless she went into that same metropolis. Finally, after she got out of the heavy traffic she stopped at a gas station and asked where she had gone wrong. With some direction she went back to the freeway and took the right exit. She had to drive right through the expressways again to get where she was going.

When she arrived at the courtroom it was abandoned all, but for a bailiff. He told her that court was over. Sandra could see that. She didn't know what to do next so she took a shot in the dark. She asked the bailiff about Drägo's case, hoping he might remember Drägo's name or something. Sandra thought she detected a slight sour note in the man's voice when he told her that Drägo had been released about a half hour earlier. She felt relieved and disappointed all at the same time.

Sandra wandered out of the courthouse into the bustling streets of the city wondering what she should do. She looked in both directions of the street. She saw a thriving metropolis with many restaurants and businesses. A thought came to her. Then she knew where to find Drägo.

He had always had a hearty appetite. Since he had been in jail for a few days, he would appreciate something other than prison food. She started walking down the busy street looking for him in every restaurant she came across. She felt like a timid puppy that had lost its owner when she questioned waitresses giving them Drägo's description. She wanted to be sure she hadn't missed him. Women always remembered Drägo. She didn't think he would have walked very far before he appeased his appetite. The police had picked him up at home, so he didn't have a car with him. She walked into the fourth restaurant on her route. Drägo was sitting at a table eating. He was stunned to see her when she walked up to the table.

"How the hell did you find me?" he asked, her visibly shocked.

"I know how much you like your food," she said, smiling and pleased with herself.

"This is incredible that you found me in this city. You know me very well. Don't you?" Drägo said, looking at her in amazement. "I'm sure glad you didn't listen to me about not coming to court because I was just sitting here thinking I might have to steal a car to get home."

After that he was often heard telling the story of how Sandra had amazed him that day and that he appreciated how well she proved to know him.

Drägo had been charged with a vague charge of attempted theft of a vehicle. He told the judge that if he had wanted to steal the vehicle the police saw him standing beside he could have had the door unlocked and the car started within three minutes. He said he wouldn't have been just standing beside it. The judge declared a recess and then him, Drägo and two bailiffs went out into the courthouse parking lot where the judge's car was parked. The judge told Drägo to prove what he claimed then looked at his watch. Drägo proved it. In less than three minutes he had the judge's car door unlocked and the engine running. The officials were shocked. The case was dismissed.

Susan and Sandra got back to Drägo's mother's house around nine in the evening from their road trip. Drägo and his mother were concerned about them because they were so late getting back.

Fortunately the trip back to Riverside was uneventful. Drägo and Sandra drove. Susan used her airline ticket. Sandra called Bill after Drägo dropped her at her apartment and went home himself.

Within a week of getting back from the trip, Sandra's uncle that she had visited during the trip called her. That was unusual because he rarely called her. Sandra found the reason for his call to be extremely unusual as well when he told her of events of the past week. A retired police officer that he was acquainted with had paid him a visit. The man wanted to know where Uncle Dan got the money to buy his new van. Dan wasn't known to have a lot of money. He worked as a bartender in a small town hotel. The retired officer said he was aware of Sandra's visit and proceeded to tell Dan everywhere that Susan and Sandra had gone. He said they went to visit Susan's father and then spent the next day in the major metropolis. Dan asked Sandra if her and Susan had gone for lunch in a revolving restaurant. Sandra said they did. Dan told her that she had left a hundred dollar bill on the table. He said their every move had been observed. Sandra was astounded and angry. Why were her and Susan followed? They were not criminals.

Bill should know the answer to that, she thought.

Sandra called him as soon as she hung up from the conversation with her uncle. Bill denied any knowledge of her and Susan being followed. He said he didn't know of any orders for anything like it. He told her that if the police wanted to have her followed they wouldn't have brought someone out of retirement to do it. That made sense to Sandra, but she knew that her and her daughter had definitely been tracked, hundred-dollar bill and all. Bill asked if it was possible that Drägo might have hired someone to follow them. Sandra told him that was ridiculous and asked why Drägo would be bothered to do that. Bill said he didn't know other than the fact that Drägo might be onto her. He didn't really think so because Drägo certainly would have had a different reaction than having her followed. Bill seemed to be as mystified as Sandra by it all. She had to let it go because she couldn't prove anything, nor would Bill admit otherwise. She remembered a time when Bill had told her if Drägo questioned her about anything she had done, she should use a technique police officers had drilled into them during their training. Deny, deny, deny! Why would he use that technique on Sandra?

Sandra had no choice but to let the incident go, but never forgot about it. She had to concern herself with the issue at hand. She was back into the thick of the investigation. She had appreciated the rest as much as the surveillance team had.

She called Bill at home a few times when she had to reach him and he wasn't on shift, which was seldom. He told her once that the overtime bill was really wracking up. Bill's wife never hesitated when she heard Sandra's voice on the phone. She either got Bill to the phone right away or told Sandra which number to call to reach him.

Bill had spent so much time on the road with the surveillance team that his wife was fed up and told him one day, "If you don't catch that asshole soon you will be answering to me instead of your supervisor."

Bill repeated what his wife had said to Sandra.

In a fleeting moment, Sandra wondered, *how much does the wife know about the case and about me?*

She never asked Bill. She dismissed the small nagging question as irrelevant. All she was concerned about was that the longer it took the police to catch Drägo, the more the chances were of him putting two and two together. He was a brilliant man. She had been into the thick of the investigation for months by that time. She didn't know how much longer she could go on living with one foot in each camp because she was operating completely against her nature. She had always been honest to a fault until it came to dealings regarding Drägo's career.

Chapter Four

On the same day as Sandra had led the police to the stolen stash of money, she also took them to the wooded area that Drägo had mysteriously pointed out to her. The stick personality was still driving. The dead end road was a quagmire of mud.

Randy looked at Bill from behind the steering wheel and said, "If we get stuck, you're pushing."

Sandra thought he might have tried to be funny. But no, the look on his face said that he was dead serious.

When they stopped at the site at the edge of the woods Bill said again, "Yes, Sandra, you were right. A camera would have been a good idea."

He was trying to draw the site where the tree stood that had been shown to Sandra. There were many trees. Sandra didn't bother to comment. Someone had seen the error of his ways. She knew that snappy "I told you so's" were never necessary. Situations always proved themselves.

Drägo went on a binge of a crime-spree soon after he pointed out the tree to Sandra. She knew then why he made a special effort to know where she should look if he was caught. He had done it so no one else would benefit from the proceeds of his crimes. Sandra would have never benefited either. She wanted nothing to do with it. It didn't matter how much money was lying around, she would have felt like an accomplice if she touched it.

The law was frantic over Drägo's heightened flurry of activity. They watched him break into many rural businesses, five and six in one night. They had to catch him red-handed because he never left any evidence behind. They were glued to his tail. The police used infrared cameras to navigate in the dark with their headlights turned off. Bill said it was tricky and they almost hit another car one night. Drägo had told Sandra that he did several jobs in a night, but Sandra didn't believe him. She thought he was boasting trying to let her think that he was better than what he was. He told her that the pickings were pretty slim for a lowly safecracker, as he put it, sometimes as well. Sometimes there was only fifty dollars in a safe. The police told Sandra that Drägo hadn't been boasting. He was telling her the truth. She had heard so much bullshit come out of Drägo's mouth in prior years that she never knew when he was telling her the truth.

Bill called Sandra in the middle of the night one time. Susan had answered the phone in her bedroom and went to her mother's room to wake her up. Bill was very excited and agitated. Susan was upset. She was very accustomed to Bill calling, but knew that something dire was up for him to call in the middle of the night.

"We had him, but he got away!" Bill told Sandra. "If he shows up at your apartment, phone my supervisor. I'm away out in the boondocks. There will be nothing I can do about it from here."

"Oh my gawd, Bill. I just can't believe this. He won't show up here," Sandra told him. "He knows this is one of the first places you would look for him."

Bill sounded defeated grasping at straws when he replied, "I know, but you know what to do if he does."

Susan had listened to Sandra's side of the conversation.

"Mom, what if they shoot him?" she asked, close to tears.

Sandra could see that her daughter was upset, fearing for Drägo's life.

"They won't shoot him, Susan, because he's not armed. They know that," Sandra said.

"They might, Mom, they're desperate!" Susan said.

"If they do it will only be in the leg, just enough to stop him," she told her daughter, trying not to let her own concern show.

Sandra wondered who on the team would be a sharp shooter. No one. She wanted to cry as well but had to keep a grip on herself for

Susan's sake.

In the beginning of the whole charade, Sandra feared the possibility of Drägo eventually getting gunned down. As Susan, she worried about the desperation the police displayed. She had worked hard to convince the police that Drägo would never be carrying a gun or any other kind of weapon. They knew from his record that he never had, but they were concerned that he might start. They asked Sandra about it several times. She always told them the same thing, it would never happen.

Finally Sandra got pissed off with constantly being asked that question and said, "He will not! He's not out to hurt anyone!"

Sandra saw an eyebrow rise so she continued talking. "Well, not physically anyway. I know that he can bankrupt a company within ten minutes, but he has never hurt anyone in the process. His life's passion is piles of money, but he won't start brandishing a weapon to get it. A woman walked into a business early one morning and caught Drägo just about to light his blowtorch. She didn't realize she had stumbled across a safe cracker until she found out later that her boss hadn't called an exterminator. She said "good morning" to Drägo. He said "good morning" and then left the building as the woman carried on about her business in a back room."

Drägo relayed the story to Sandra as if he was astonished.

Another woman had come up behind Drägo catching him in the act of robbing her business and asked, "What the hell are you doing?"

The woman frightened Drägo who just took off.

When Drägo told Sandra about it he said, "Imagine the nerve of that women! If I had been an armed robber she could have been killed coming up behind me like that."

Bill still expressed concern about one of the team getting hurt.

"You have us pretty much convinced that Drägo will not carry a weapon, but what about the blow torch he always uses to get into the safes? Do you think he might turn that on one of us?" Bill asked Sandra.

"If he is startled, I guess that could happen," she said. "Sure he could turn around when the torch is lit, yes, but it wouldn't be a deliberate attempt to hurt anyone. It would just be a knee jerk reaction because somebody scared the shit out of him. He hates someone coming up behind him unannounced at any time. Cripes, he almost jumped two feet in the air one day ready to take flight when my water cooler gurgled behind him. Still he didn't stab it with a knife within reach on the kitchen counter."

Bill and the rest of the investigating team were always amazed by how well Sandra knew Drägo. The woman wanted to make sure the police had no justification to shoot to kill an unarmed man, allowing no room for error. She was very adamant when they needed convincing of anything. Bill always asked for Sandra's opinion regarding Drägo as to what he may or may not do.

Sandra didn't know that the police had been shooting over Drägo's head before Bill called her in the middle of the night. When she found out later that morning she didn't tell Susan. That was all the girl needed to hear to cause her to completely crumble under the stress. As it was Susan was concerned for her mother's safety as well. She didn't feel that the police were being careful enough to protect Sandra. Susan said they were only concerned about getting their man. She called Bill and balled him out about that one day. Bill assured her that their first priority was Sandra's protection. Susan still had her doubts about that. She had never trusted Bill. She had never met him either.

Sandra wondered how she was supposed to call Bill's supervisor if Drägo got to her apartment. She didn't dare make that kind of a call with Drägo being within earshot. She didn't bother to say that to Bill because he was already agitated. Sandra dismissed the thought because she knew Drägo wasn't stupid. What about Bill though? He claimed that he ate, drank and slept Drägo, so shouldn't he know more about the man than what he did?

The surveillance team had followed Drägo into a small rural town as always. Bill got within a few inches of touching Drägo to place him under arrest. He had come up behind Drägo catching him inside a business and called him by name. Sandra was sure it would have been before the torch was lit. Drägo turned to look at Bill and then lit into flight out of the business he was about to rob. A chase ensued over ice and snow. The team was slipping and sliding. Drägo seemed to have grown wings on his heels according to Bill. Drägo ran as if jet propelled unhindered by the slippery terrain. Bill commented that Drägo was obviously in good shape for his age. He outran the entire team of police officers. He said he had never seen anyone run that fast. Sandra told him that was because Drägo practiced running with his dog. Drägo could keep up to the dog. Sandra had watched some of those practice sessions. Steve told her the reasoning behind running with the dog. Sandra shook her head realizing that Drägo couldn't even play with the dog without there being an illicit reason for it. Bill also told Sandra that shooting over Drägo's head demanding he stop didn't faze him. It just made him run faster.

"He's just not afraid!" Bill exclaimed to Sandra, still absolutely amazed.

"Yes, he is afraid!" Sandra said emphatically. "He's scared shitless, but that just means that he can run faster than you can because he has that extra rush of adrenaline that fear gives us all. You know what they say about being able to run faster scared than mad. It's obviously true. Don't forget he was the only one out there who thought he was running for his life."

Bill agreed although he admitted to having a good rush of adrenaline himself. He was sitting at Sandra's kitchen table looking exhausted after the hullabaloo of the night before. He was wearing a tensor bandage on his wrist. He had fallen on the ice the night before during the chase and sprained it. He said the entire team was falling down. Those who did manage to maneuver on the ice didn't get very far because they soon tripped and fell over their fallen comrades. Drägo had evaded them again. Sandra shook her head in disbelief although even in her dismay she almost laughed. It sounded to her like a scene from a cartoon. She imagined cops sliding into a frustrated heap one on top of the other while Drägo ran for his life. The tangled web had become even more tangled.

When Drägo relayed that evening's events to Sandra, days later, he described it as a "harrowing experience." He didn't mention the gunshots fired because he knew that would upset Sandra. His facial expressions as he talked told her that he thought the police were shooting to kill. She hated to let him believe that anyone was actually out to kill him. She wished she could tell him different.

After that, Bill told Steve to be very careful because he looked so much like his father.

If a cop should stick a gun in his face he was told to throw his hands in the air and yell, "It's not me you're looking for, it's my dad."

Steve was told it could happen easily because not only did they look alike, but even their very distinctive walk was the same. Sandra told Steve to quit wearing one of his dad's jackets that he liked to wear because it made him more of a target than what he already was. Susan had often commented on the uncanny similarities between Drägo and Steve.

At ten years old Susan said, "Mom, he's so much like Drägo! Look at the way his eyes squint when he laughs. Look at the way he stands, walks and talks. Everything is just like Drägo!"

"Yes, I know, Susan. Isn't that something?" her mother said.

Chapter Five

Years earlier, and one jail term earlier before Sandra became involved in the capture of Steve's father, one entire rural police department couldn't handle the chase. Being a small station they didn't have the manpower for one thing. Every member would have had to dedicate every shift toward the capture of Drägo leaving no one to look after their small community. None of the small force had the expertise needed either. They tried for a few months before they exhausted themselves and called for reinforcements from their headquarters.

A team of eight under cover police officers rallied in the small town where the family lived. Sandra was contacted by two of them. They wanted to pick her brain. They didn't approach her until they had checked her out thoroughly with people who she had close association with. Sandra was deemed credible. The police hoped to recruit her as help.

When the law approached her, Sandra had known Drägo for twenty-two years. He had spent all of those years in and out of prison. Sandra had lived with him and born his child, Steve. Susan was three months old when Sandra met Drägo.

In the four years the family lived together they appeared to be a typical young family making their way quite nicely in life with a bright future ahead. It seemed the only thing that was missing was a white picket fence. There was a flaw in their perfect looking lives. The man Sandra and her children loved would not put his expertise to rest. She prayed for the comforts of their own home and the responsibilities of parenting to sway Drägo's illegal tendencies. That never happened.

Although Drägo held an excellent paying job and Sandra went back to work when Steve was two, there was just never enough cash flow to satisfy the criminal mind. Cash was still stolen from many businesses in the area and beyond. Sometimes it was spent frivolously to impress people. Other times it paid the milkman.

Sandra remembers the time when Steve and Susan were babies and she was standing at the front door talking to the milkman and telling him she didn't have any money to pay for the week's milk. Drägo was listening to her talk to the milkman. She heard the back door open and close. She thought Drägo had left the house for some reason. A minute later he appeared behind her at the front door and handed the milkman the money he was owed.

Sandra questioned him about where the money had come from because he had said before that he didn't have any money. She could see that Drägo didn't want to tell her. She kept questioning him and asked why she heard him go out the back door. Reluctantly he said he had to go to the car. Sandra had excellent hearing. Steve referred to it as "mother hearing" later in his life. Drägo wasn't aware of her keen hearing until then. Sandra wanted to know why he had to go to the car. What did that have to do with him showing up at the front door with money, she asked him. Drägo could see that she wasn't going to give up until she got a straight answer. Finally he said he got the money out of the flashlight in the car. Sandra looked at him with a bewildered look on her face waiting for an explanation. She had visions, but she wanted to hear it come out of Drägo's mouth. He said he had taken the batteries out of the flashlight and replaced them with a roll of money so the police wouldn't find it if they searched his car. Sandra looked at him and shook her head. Nothing more was said about it.

Sandra had a passion for red velvet drapes and ended up being sorry she had ever mentioned it to Drägo the one time she did. They appeared in their living room that year for her birthday, wall to wall. Sandra was sad instead of elated. Drägo couldn't understand why she wasn't thrilled with her gift. The drapes were more beautiful than she could have ever imagined, but she knew they had been purchased with stolen money. She didn't want them. Sandra ended up giving the drapes to a woman who had only plastic curtains to adorn her windows. The woman didn't know they had been purchased with stolen money. Sandra never told her. She wanted her to be able to enjoy them as she couldn't.

In the years Sandra spent with Drägo, she had many occasions to wonder what life really had in store for her and her children. The future looked bleak. Sandra also felt she could easily become a basket case. One of Drägo's antics that became a common occurrence was disappearing in the night. It is difficult to be a daytime burglar unless the thief is armed. Sandra used to awaken at least once a week to find herself alone in bed. She never managed to hear his departure. Drägo was getting good, well practiced. Just before dawn, after lying in wait, Sandra would hear him slipping quietly through the back door making his way to the kitchen table where he would proceed to lay out the evening's work for counting.

On one occasion, Sandra deliberately walked downstairs and interrupted his counting. The kitchen table was covered with piles of neatly stacked bills. She had never seen so much money in one place before. Drägo was stunned when Sandra appeared. It was like an unspoken law of the household had been broken. She had little to say, but was thinking lots. She watched him meticulously count and sort the money. The total tally was eight hundred dollars. That was a lot of money in those days. She watched him put the money in a spot too high for her to reach in the cupboards. He became paranoid of letting Sandra see where he hid his stash. The look on her face revealed exactly what she was thinking. That was the last time she witnessed the counting of any money. It was gone when she went to retrieve it much later in the day. Drägo had guessed exactly what her plans were.

He eyed her warily when he stashed the cash and said, "I don't know if I should let you see where I am putting this because you might do something stupid like burn it."

Were her thoughts that easily read? Defacing national currency, or whatever the illegalities are, Sandra didn't give a damn. Burn it she would have if it had still been where she had seen it stashed. Drägo said the money had been stolen to buy a nineteen sixty-five mustang for Sandra. She guessed that he thought he could buy her approval of what he was doing. After all he was doing it for her, or so he pointed out. Sandra's punishment for not being trusted was not receiving the gift. That was fortunate because it would have been a crime to have to give it away and a bigger crime to keep it. Besides, Sandra had seen the car. It was the wrong color. It was baby blue, not candy apple red. She also suspected that the car was stolen property because the deal regarding it was so secretive. The vehicle was in a paint shop, freshly painted when Sandra saw it. She didn't trust the people who had done the work and couldn't help but wonder why the car was offered for sale to Drägo. It certainly wasn't a vehicle she would ever drive or have her name on the ownership papers.

Life carried on day by day with mounting dread. The law picked Drägo up on several occasions, but he always came back a free man. On one of those occasions, Drägo and Sandra had one of many arguments about his criminal lifestyle. She took the children and left the house after he went to sleep. He had been up since the wee hours of the morning.

Sandra knew there was something amiss that particular time because Drägo didn't come home until a few hours after dawn.

What is he doing out there in the daylight? she wondered. *It's just not like him.*

She was so sure of something being wrong that she was surprised to see Drägo come home at all. She was convinced that she wouldn't hear from him again until he called from a jail.

When Sandra took the kids to leave the apartment, she got to the car and found the wiring all ripped out from under the dash. That only meant one thing to her. The car had been hot wired, as Drägo called it. She saw the car had been ransacked as well. The keys were not in the ignition as she thought they would be. She had quietly searched Drägo's pockets for them in their bedroom, but hadn't found them.

Sandra went back into the apartment and woke Drägo up asking him where the car keys were. He was sleeping like he was dead. Finally he woke up enough to mumble that he had lost them.

"Really," Sandra said, not believing him because he was a very careful person. "Then I guess it was you that ransacked the car looking for them!"

Drägo didn't answer her.

"Have you completely lost your mind?" she asked him.

"Don't you know that there is all kinds of identification in the glove compartment?" she asked him.

"The police would have seen that," she told him.

She had wondered before that day why he would leave it there instead of destroying it.

Drägo still didn't answer her. He was sleeping again. Sandra left the bedroom and phoned the local garage where their other car was in for repairs. She asked if it was ready to be picked up. It was. She asked if someone could bring the car to her because she didn't want to walk to the garage with the kids. Susan was just over a year old. Steve was a month old. It was winter time. The garage owner brought the car to her. Sandra didn't have money for a taxi.

Soon after Sandra's departure, the city police arrived and let themselves into the apartment with Drägo's keys in hand. They walked into the bedroom and woke Drägo up. They took him away. He wasn't home when Sandra got back to the apartment later in the day. The car was there. She was home for about two hours, worried sick, when Drägo walked in the door.

She was considerably calmer than what she had been that morning. She asked Drägo what was going on. He said he had hot wired the car to get home because the police had discovered it left with its engine running in a back alley behind a local business. Drägo had been going to rob the business, but had to run when he saw the police at his car. Sandra asked why he would do something as stupid as leave the car running behind a business he was going to rob. He said he did that because it was cold out and he didn't want to have to go back to a cold car.

The police had locked the car up and pocketed the keys. That didn't stop Drägo for more than a few hours. He climbed up on a roof a good distance away, but within sight of the vehicle. From his vantage point he watched the police multiply into a large search party almost immediately. He watched them until their huge manhunt became man less. After a considerable amount of time the manhunt dwindled to regular patterns of patrols. During one of those patrols, Drägo's car was reported missing. He drove home unnoticed in the morning rush hour traffic.

"You wouldn't believe the number of cop cars that were there!" he told Sandra with obvious amazement.

He thought it was quite a trip and was proud of himself for eluding the dragnet.

The police never had enough evidence to hold Drägo. All they had were their keen suspicions that were useless in a courtroom. They often kept what they hoped would become material evidence, grasping at straws. Drägo often returned home with no coat. The police seemed to always take a particular liking to his shoes as well. That explained why he began asking Sandra for empty bread bags in the wintertime. When put over shoes or boots no discernible footprints are left behind. It took Sandra a while to catch onto that trick. The authorities never did.

The police were desperate. When the children were toddlers, they tried pumping them for their last names. The kids were two and three years old. The visitors who wore matching uniforms intrigued them. After all, they must have been friends of Daddy's because they often came to the door. Daddy often went out to play with them.

The police were standing inside at the back entrance way to the house. Of course they had come for Drägo, whom they allowed to go upstairs before he left the house with them. Drägo claimed he wanted to change his shirt. Sandra found out later that he had a wad of money on him that he wanted to stash away. In the meantime, the kids stood there looking at "Daddy's friends" admiring their uniforms. Sandra's attempt to take them away from the entrance way was foiled by one officer who got the bright idea of chatting with the little tykes.

"Hi," he smiled at Susan, "What's your name"?

"Susan," she smiled back at him.

"Oh, that's a nice name. Is this your brother?" he indicated Steve.

"Yes," she said.

"What's his name?" the officer asked.

"Steve," Susan told him.

The cop watched Sandra closely and saw that she wasn't going to interfere in his conversation with her daughter. She wasn't impressed by the tactic, but she didn't see any harm in it either. The cop continued talking to Susan.

"What's your last name, Susan?" he asked her.

"Susan," she told him with a shy little grin of a three year old.

"Oh. What's Steve's last name?" he asked her not quite so chipper anymore.

"Steve," Susan said, still smiling in appreciation of the attention the officer was giving her and her brother.

Sandra caught Drägo coming down the stairs and told him that the police were pumping the kids for their last names. Drägo didn't show any concern. He shrugged his shoulders at Sandra and went to the door to go out and play. Sandra was a bit baffled by his reaction. Drägo told the kids he would be back soon. The police officers glanced at one another when they heard that.

The old adage "out of the mouths of babes" didn't help the police at all. The kids didn't know their last names. They didn't even know there was such a thing as a last name. It was a subject that deliberately never came up because their last names were different. Even if the kids had known their last names it wouldn't have helped the police at all. That is the only reason Sandra allowed the friendly gentle interrogation of her daughter to continue.

Drägo returned home a few hours later. Playtime was over. Sandra noticed the look on his face that had become all too familiar to her. He was looking quite smug.

"They don't have anything on me," he told her. "They never do."

Sandra didn't bother to comment. Drägo was right. Sandra just shook her head at the incredibility of it all.

Chapter Six

Sandra recalls a particular day shortly after that when Drägo had picked her up at work. It was a civic holiday. Sandra had to work but Drägo didn't, so he had been home all day with the kids who were in the back seat of the car. Steve whimpered to his mother and reached toward her with both arms outstretched for her to take him as soon as she got into the car.

Sandra went to do exactly that but stopped when Drägo said, "Leave him in the back."

It was a demand. Sandra saw fear in her son's eyes. His eyes pleaded for her to take him into the front with her. Susan had an odd look on her face as well but said nothing.

"What's wrong with the kids?" Sandra asked Drägo.

"Oh, Steve and I had a bit of a run-in today," he told her.

"How come?" She asked.

"Because he pissed his pants," Drägo said.

"Hmm," was all Sandra said.

Sandra thought she would have to get more serious about toilet training Steve. The subject was dropped, but not forgotten. When the family got home, Sandra took the kids outside to play. They were playing with a big ball on the sidewalk in front of the house.

Steve fell on his bum and said, "Hurts, Mom." Tears formed in his eyes. Sandra didn't think he had fallen that hard. She picked him up and comforted him anyway. The tears went away as Steve clung to his mother.

Susan watched this and said, "Daddy spanked Steve today."

Sandra said, "Yes, I heard."

She was still holding Steve and cuddled him closer thinking about what Susan had said.

After dinner that evening, Sandra took both of the kids upstairs for their bath. She couldn't believe what she saw when she undressed Steve. His backside was black and blue from his mid back almost down to his knees. Sandra was aghast. She picked up Steve and headed down the stairs with him screaming Drägo's name.

"What is this?" she screamed at Drägo putting Steve's bare butt into full view.

Drägo started to approach Sandra and his son.

"Stay away from us," she screamed again, backing up the stairs holding her son.

Steve flinched at the sight of his father's approach. He sobbed and clung to his mother as if he was hanging on for his life. He was terrified of his father.

Sandra tried soothing him telling him, "It's ok. Nobody is going to hurt you again."

"I told you that Steve and I had a run-in today," Drägo said, wearing his sickening smug look.

"Do you call this a run-in? I call it child abuse!" Sandra screamed again.

"Well...he pissed his pants," Drägo said as if that justified his actions.

"He's only two years old, for gawd sake!" Sandra screamed.

"He still shouldn't be pissing his pants," Drägo said, trying to pull rank.

Sandra told Drägo that her and the kids would be leaving. He told her that she wouldn't be going anywhere. Then he changed his mind. She could go, but she couldn't take her children with her.

In a threatening tone Drägo said, "You're not going anywhere with them. But I can pick up both of them right now and you will never see them again."

"You might be able to take Steve, but you can't take Susan," she spit at him, "because she's not yours!"

Sandra had taken a helluva risk and was terrified that Drägo would wrestle her son from her arms. Mother and child held onto each other as if their lives depended on it. Their lives did. The look on Drägo's face turned from threatening to one of surprise. He had never thought of Susan as being anything, but Sandra's alone, as if a father just didn't exist.

"I can take Steve! He's mine!" he countered Sandra after a moment of thought.

"Prove it!" Sandra dared, the words spitting out of her mouth.

Drägo was dumbfounded. Sandra surprised herself by saying that, but she immediately got over it. She had learned early in life that if someone was pointing a cannon at her there was no point in aiming a sling shot back. Drägo's chin seemed to drop to the floor. Sandra was glaring at him with a menacing glare. She could see that Drägo was absolutely stunned. It took a few seconds for him to regain his composure and mask his shock.

"Steve and I just have to go to a hospital and have blood tests taken. That will prove he his is my son," he told Sandra with a cocky confidence in his voice.

The smug look had returned. Drägo knew that Steve definitely was his son. The child looked too much like him to not be fathered by him.

"Are you telling me that you are the only man in this world with your type of blood?" Sandra dared to spit back at him.

She wasn't afraid anymore. She knew she had him with a statement like that. Drägo's facial expression changed instantly from cocky to that of the bewildered. He had to think about that for a minute. A deep frown furrowed his brow. Just then Sandra's cousin knocked on the front door and walked into the house. Sandra was standing half way down the stairway in plain view of the front door still clinging to Steve. Her opportunity to get help had just arrived. She turned Steve's bare backside towards the door and told her cousin to go home and call the police. Her cousin was obviously shocked at the sight as well.

"I don't want to get involved," her cousin said, hanging his head as he turned back towards the door.

He glanced back over his shoulder at Sandra and said, "I'm sorry."

With that he closed the door behind himself as he left the house. Sandra was stunned and furious all at the same time. Drägo got cocky again.

"Nice try, but you can see that even your own cousin won't help you," he said with an evil smirk on his face and the attitude of "See, you're the only one who thinks I did anything wrong."

"That's ok." Sandra said. "Don't let that make you think you are going to get away with this. If you sleep in this house tonight you had better sleep damn lightly because I will put a knife right through you!"

Drägo didn't doubt that. The look on Sandra's face left nothing to the imagination. No one was going to get away with abusing her children. Drägo left the house shortly after that.

Sandra and the children slept in the same bed that night. Sandra barely slept because she was listening for the deliberately closed bedroom door to open. The opening of the closed door could be the only alarm she would have even with her keen hearing. When Sandra got up during the night to go to the bathroom, she realized she had another alarm system. The large family dog had parked himself on the floor outside the bedroom door. She almost tripped over him. Sandra spent a couple of minutes loving him up and telling him what a good boy he was. The dog soaked it all up. Sandra thought he looked pleased with himself and so he should have been. When she got back into bed with the children, she heard the dog settle himself on the floor again right up against the closed door. Sandra smiled and fell into a sound sleep.

Drägo had threatened to take the kids because he knew that their children were everything to Sandra. Making that kind of threat was also his way of telling her that she shouldn't entertain any ideas of reporting him to the authorities for the abuse or anything else that he was up to. It was unlikely that Drägo would take Susan since Sandra had reminded him that Susan wasn't his child, but he might. He would take Steve. Sandra couldn't let that thought intimidate her. People had to know what Drägo had done to Steve. That was the only way Sandra could hope to prevent him from taking Steve. She knew there were places she had to get to. Her son's well being hinged on his mother's determination.

After breakfast the following morning, Sandra dressed the kids and they all headed out to catch a city bus. There was no second family car at the time because Drägo didn't buy the mustang. Sandra watched carefully for any sign of Drägo while they waited for the bus. There was no sign of him.

The mother and children boarded a bus. Their first stop was the hospital. Sandra reported the abuse to her doctor. She went to the headquarters of the local police department and filed the same report. From there she was going to Child and Family Services(CFS). The police officer she talked to offered to call CFS and have them come to the station and talk to Sandra in his office. She was grateful for the suggestion because her and the kids had been on the bus most of the morning by that time. Sandra had to get everything on record, many records, because of Drägo's threat. She was aware that he was perfectly capable of grabbing both kids, or at least Steve and running. Sandra also knew that the police would not be able to find him. She didn't even know if they would try. Her kids would be gone, quite possibly for years until the police managed to catch Drägo red handed on an unrelated charge. Sandra couldn't let that happen to Steve or Susan.

At the time of reporting the beating, Sandra informed the police of some very important information that would have solved the mystery that had haunted them for years. Who was this man who had no criminal record, but was so good at what he did? In her own mind, Sandra wanted Drägo to be caught because that might be her only escape, but no, the police didn't hear or comprehend what she was telling them. She told them to be aware of a certain surname if her son ever disappeared. She spelled the name to an officer. He wrote it down. He had written down Drägo's last name before that in the abuse report. She established with the police that Drägo would in fact be charged with kidnapping if her son ever disappeared.

"It's one thing to say he would be charged, but would he actually be pursued?" Sandra asked the officer.

"Yes, he would be because you and him have never been married. A common-law father has no legal rights to children born from the union," he told her.

Sandra wasn't consoled very much by that information because she had seen how Drägo could evade the law. However, it did let her know that she had a legal leg to stand on if it ever happened that either one or both of her children went missing. Everything was on official records.

Three nights later, Sandra woke up to the dog making a helluva ruckus. Somebody was downstairs. She ran and got both kids from their beds and took them into her room. There was a phone in there. She was just beginning to wonder whether she should call the police or not. It could be Drägo, which could be all the more reason for an emergency call. Then she realized the dog was at the top of the stairs barking at someone on the stairway. She flipped on the hallway light switch. Drägo was standing on the third stair from the top and the dog was snapping and snarling at him. Sandra called the dog off. Drägo stood there looking very sheepish. He told Sandra that the dog wouldn't let him up the stairs.

"That's because the dog knows what you did to Steve," Sandra told Drägo. "He is protecting us from you."

Drägo hung his head and sobbed, "I know. I'm sorry."

"It's Steve you need to apologize to," Sandra said.

Drägo did apologize to Steve. The little boy was happy to have his dad back. Regardless of the sincere apology, the children were never left alone with Drägo again—even for a five minute trip to the corner store. Arguments often ensued over that, but Sandra didn't care. She wanted Drägo to have a constant reminder of what he did to Steve. It was her way of letting him know that he would not get another opportunity to repeat the abuse. He would have to come through her first.

Unlike the present day, Child and Family Services were of no help. The social worker expressed sympathy for Sandra and her kids, but offered little consolation and just said she would speak to Drägo. She did speak to Drägo who walked away from the interview wearing his smug look. The advocate simply told him that beating up his son wasn't a nice thing to do. That told Sandra for sure that she would have no allies in CFS. That didn't surprise her. She only went to them to make an official report that she knew had to be filed and held on record for many years. Could Sandra rely on the police either because hadn't they repeatedly proven over the years that they couldn't catch Drägo? It was a dim thought to know that she not only had to protect her children from Drägo's criminal life, but physical abuse as well. Life was a constantly accelerating war of wits.

Chapter Seven

The young mother had way too many things to think about. One of the many things she thought about was the irony that life had never been easy for her. It hadn't been Sandra's first encounter with CFS. It hadn't been the first time she had seen the organization be as good as useless either. Fortunately the organization takes a zero tolerance attitude on child abuse in the present day. That didn't help Sandra and her children at the time.

Sandra thought about another time in her struggle to survive life. Her grandmother, who despised her, had taken over raising her when her parents separated when she was two. She was eleven when she went to live with her father and his second family. It was an attempt to get away from the mental anguish her grandmother lavishly dished out to her. She had been a well-behaved child, but regardless, in nine years, she hadn't been able to design a behavior to avoid her grandmother's wrath, nor to meet her approval.

Sandra had walked into another family completely unprepared for what took place over the next five years. She had become the oldest child of five with a domineering stepmother. Of course the domination wasn't much different than her former life. Sandra's heart sank when she saw it for the first time. She knew she was going to have to keep her wits about her.

Already established in her independence, Sandra decided that because she could look after herself she could certainly help to look after the other four children who were a definite handful for any one person. She spent years believing that showing that kind of maturity, beyond her years, was a mistake.

She spent the rest of her life saying, "It never pays to be too smart because then you are expected to know everything."

As a child, she didn't realize that an eleven year old couldn't be held responsible for the mistakes of toxic parents. No more than a two year old could. She didn't know how to design an acceptable behavior once more.

Desperate to be accepted into the family and prove her worth, she took it upon herself to undertake as many responsibilities as she could. She hoped that initiative would show that she was worth something after all. Those responsibilities included doing most of the household chores, usually while baby-sitting her siblings. When those duties started, Sandra was eleven years old. Her youngest newborn sibling was only two weeks old. Sandra soon became the live-in baby-sitter/ housekeeper earning her keep. She was seldom seen without four very small children crowded around her, hence the nickname, "Mini-Mom" as she was known in the small town on a sandy shore of Lake Minton. Sandra's stepmother usually suggested that she ask a friend to come for the weekend when it was known that Sandra would be left overnight with the five children. It wasn't long before friends caught onto the ploy and didn't want to be there anymore because they didn't want to help Sandra baby-sit. After one telephone conversation with her father's boss, the man asked how old Sandra was. Her father lied saying she was fifteen.

It became very clear by the time Sandra was twelve that when the laundry or floors needed attention, it was her attention they needed. Naturally, those chores were in addition to everything else that demanded her attention. Sandra's father wore green work uniforms all the time. He never failed to point out any of her expected duties while he complained that she had burnt the potatoes for dinner again. It was a nasty habit she had. Sometimes she thought it might have been a small act of rebellion on her part. Sandra knew how her father hated eating those burnt potatoes. She got so she didn't mind them at all. Her taste buds reveled in quietly devouring the vengeance.

About that same time, Mother Nature noticed how quickly Sandra was growing up and decided she might just as well look the part. Right at that time and place sprouting into a young woman wasn't a good thing. She didn't take long to blossom. It didn't take long for her father to notice either. She became a twelve-year-old woman living under siege of being sexually attacked by her father.

After he had made a couple of visits to Sandra's bedroom, as if he knew exactly when her bra would be off, she realized what she was dealing with. The first time could have been accidental. She thought not. The leer was present. There was no mistaking the second time for what it was. That time she was fondled and kissed as if she was his lover instead of his daughter. Sandra was in shock. She didn't know what to do. When she flinched at his advances, he asked her if she was concerned that the neighbor's son might be upset if he knew what was happening. The boy and her had managed to become friends, but they were only twelve! The question came as an accusation riddled with jealousy.

At the same time it was made clear to Sandra that there was no need for her stepmother to know of what was happening in her bedroom. No different than any other child in the same position, she reluctantly agreed because she was afraid to do otherwise. Sandra's father projected his guilt of the sexual advances by holding her responsible for her stepmother not finding out, burdening a child with the secret and the shame. She couldn't believe what was happening! He was her father! Sandra feared something terrible would happen if she tried fending him off. She thought that somehow it would be turned into her fault either by her molester or his wife. Her grandmother had always degraded her saying that everything was her fault whenever anything happened in the household.

If Sandra told her stepmother she feared the woman might have left, leaving her with five children and her father, if she believed her at all. Being left alone with her father would have been a fate worse than hell. Her stepmother had already told Sandra that she intended to have a legal document written up naming her as guardian of the children as soon as she became of legal age. When Sandra dared to question the motive for such a thing her stepmother said it was protection if anything should happen between her and Sandra's father. Not if anything should happen to both of them, but if anything happened between them. She never used the words separation or divorce. Even with Sandra's lack of worldly experience she believed that she knew what the woman was saying to her. It frightened the twelve year-old-girl.

The look of insanity in her father's eyes frightened her as well. She had seen it before in his mother's eyes.

It must be hereditary, Sandra thought, *but why do they always want to hurt me*? The answer to that question seemed to lie in the fact that she was her mother's daughter. Her father and grandmother hated Sandra's mother.

According to her stepmother, her father had said, "She's just like her mother" shortly after Sandra's arrival.

Her grandmother had said those exact words when she was two. They thought of her as a budding bouquet of trouble fertilized by her mother's blood.

After several unsuccessful attempts to sway Sandra toward her father's intentions, she was introduced to alcohol since she obviously needed loosening up. The panty remover technique became one of Sandra's greatest fears. It had probably been used on many others before her although she prayed none of the victims were children. Intoxicated at thirteen, she loathed the sight of her father and dreaded the days her stepmother was occupied at her part-time job. Sandra wondered whose idea it was for the stepmother to suddenly take on employment. She hadn't worked since she started having a family.

Any attempts at being absent from the household on those days were always foiled by Sandra's father insisting he needed her to help care for the other five children. Her father would leer at her triumphantly when his wife agreed making sure that Sandra stay at home to help. He never failed to prove the real reasoning behind his claim that he couldn't look after his young children alone.

Although he hated Sandra's mini skirt, her father's attitude toward it always changed when her stepmother wasn't home. Sandra was asked to wear it on several of those occasions.

There were times when one of the small children would announce to their mother when she got home that Sandra was drunk. Of course their father had sworn them to secrecy, but everyone knows how well pre-schoolers can keep a secret. Appearing shocked with the disclosure of Sandra's condition, her stepmother still didn't question her husband about the liberal access he was allowing a thirteen year old to alcohol. Hell, he insisted she drink it. Sandra hated the alcohol, but had to take the blame for consuming it.

She realized her stepmother found it easier to ignore as if she really didn't want to know what was going on in her absence. With the dawning of that realization, Sandra was positive that she had no ally in her stepmother. Worse yet, she never would. Sandra's blossomed body screamed for someone who would believe to hear her concerns. She felt like a sacrificial lamb. No one in the household cared enough to stand in her defense. She felt dirty and worthless. Her grandmother must have been right when she used to always say that to Sandra. Feelings of repressed rage had no outlet because Sandra was never allowed to show anger without it being grounds for some form of punishment.

Sandra was unaware that there was someone else watching the situation. A lengthy discussion, of which she didn't initiate, took place between Sandra and her step-grandmother. The new grandmother wanted to know about the amount of baby-sitting that was expected of Sandra. She instructed Sandra to tell her parents that she would no longer baby-sit her siblings. That announcement brought on the crime and punishment of all time.

Sandra's soul was sliced as her beloved guitar and lessons were ripped from existence. The one and only thing she had in her life that was hers alone was no longer hers. The only time she ever had to herself, other than cutting the grass, was when she was practicing her lessons. Even at that she used to get hell for spending too much time on her lessons. The bastards had found another way to hurt her. Sandra could never let them know. The gloating look on their faces when the punishment was doled out told her that they would gloat over any suffering that showed. Alone in her room that night silent pain and helplessness rolled down Sandra's cheeks.

Her only glimmer of hope was the thought, *it can't last forever*.

By the time Sandra reached fifteen she refused to drink with her father. That made him angry, but the girl knew he had to suppress that anger as she always had to. She felt she had gained a foothold of control, but worried about how long she would be able to fend off her father. Sandra had become an obsession to him. His face wore the leer of a predator while he watched her incessantly.

There was a time when Sandra walked the entire length of the family home in a trance like state, having no recollection of it. Her younger siblings were sleeping. Sandra was baby-sitting. She remembered thinking about a bottle of vallium the doctor had prescribed for her and considering taking all of them, but she does not remember leaving the living room and walking through the house to get them. When she found herself with them in her hands in the bathroom, she snapped out of the trance she had been in for months. Who would look after the younger children? Sandra knew then that something had to change.

That is when Sandra involved Child and Family Services, in a desperate plea for the organization to remove her from her father's home. There was no doubt in her social worker's mind that her complaint was valid.

CFS took their time, but finally arrived at Sandra's home to investigate her complaint. The child knew she would be called a liar by anyone in the home when the abuse surfaced. The stepmother was jealous of Sandra's presence in her world. She became a ruthless enemy constantly on the look out for something to pin on Sandra. A small misdemeanor often became a full-blown crime. Sandra was often not aware of her conviction or crime until her father came home and was recruited as a judge. Sandra's stepmother failed to speak to her on those occasions. Being shunned was always a clue to the child that she was about to be convicted of something. The drama was always high and the exaggerations wild as the trial would unfold with fabricated evidence. Sandra couldn't understand how her stepmother could stand right in front of her and tell barefaced lies about her activities. The stepmother always appointed herself as the prosecutor and a one-woman jury claiming the verdict was "guilty as charged." A defense didn't even enter the picture. The woman truly hated her stepdaughter. In her distorted mind she was jealous of the child. Sandra would just stand there looking at the both of them wondering how they could be such beasts. They never failed to astonish her. Sandra would make sure they didn't get away with it. Patience truly is a virtue that Sandra had acquired at a young age.

As expected when confronted by Sandra's social worker, both the father and his wife claimed the girl was a liar. That verdict wasn't surprising to either Sandra or the social worker. In a fleeting glance at Sandra the look in her father's eyes was as if his daughter had betrayed him.

Sandra ended an hour-long confrontation by staring her father straight in the face and saying in a very even but accusing tone, "You and I know who's telling the truth here!"

The murderous look on her father's face proved it all. His body quaked with rage. His eyes bulged, his face reddened, neck veins appeared on the verge of bursting as he spit out denials. Sandra wasn't afraid because she had little left to lose. The stepmother was a silent partner in the abuse. The woman had always found any suspicion she had as easier to ignore than confront. Confrontation would have looked like the stepmother was standing in defense of Sandra. To avoid that she found it more appropriate to hate the child.

In the present day, such a complaint from a child would at least warrant a thorough investigation. At that time, the only help Sandra received from the society was the advice to leave home as soon as she turned sixteen. The social worker feared the guardian scenario as well. There was six months left on Sandra's tour of duty. CFS said it was obvious from her father's reaction that she wasn't fabricating the story. The man would not admit to it. Sandra had done nothing wrong to be declared a delinquent to have herself removed therefore; she was a prisoner not to be removed without her warden's consent. The woman from CFS even suggested that if Sandra did become a delinquent then the organization would be able to take her without consent.

Sandra thought, *ya, right! Isn't that cute! I am the one who has to do something wrong! Haven't my father and stepmother done enough wrong? Why do I have to become a delinquent in order to escape being a victim of sexual abuse? This whole situation stinks*!

Fortunately, children in the same situation now are dealing with completely different attitudes toward the crimes of sexual and physical abuse. Needless to say, it became too risky for Sandra's father to fulfill his fantasy. The molesting stopped, but Sandra knew she was hated even more for exposing her father's obsession.

Everyone, Sandra included, played a role of being a normal family. She knew it would soon be over. She could wait. Sandra left home three weeks after she turned sixteen. She wondered what took her so long. When the credits rolled, the finale claimed that no one could believe anything that Sandra said because she was on drugs. Her stepbrothers and sisters grew up hearing a story of track marks on their older sister's arms. To this day, records at CFS prove that Sandra's stepmother and father are the real liars. Both of them were dastardly parents. Sandra dares them to say anything different because it's never too late to go to court on charges of sexual abuse.

Chapter Eight

The authorities were baffled as to why they couldn't find a criminal record on Drägo. Sandra had told them what to look for. His record was under a completely different name. It was a name he had inherited from his stepfather. There had never been a legal adoption. Before Steve was born Drägo's stepfather told his wife to tell Drägo to take back his own name. The stepfather didn't want the child using his name because he was born out of wedlock. He was also an extremely difficult man to deal with who didn't like Sandra. He didn't like many people.

Drägo's stepfather told his wife, "I do not want her or that child using my name!"

Drägo did take back his real name so the child would bare the right one. That was the right thing to do when naming a child, but Drägo seen it as something completely different. That maneuver put as good as a void on his past record. As he told Sandra, "The cops would have to match up my fingerprints to know who I am and the chances of that are pretty slim, in fact next to impossible."

Well that's great news, she thought, knowing full well that he was stating a true fact for a change.

She shook her head again at the rationale behind everything he did. Everything was toward criminal gain. The technology wasn't good enough at the time to be able to match fingerprints. Sandra's heart sank. All hell was about to break loose.

Sandra's training throughout her childhood in determination, independence and self-defense wasn't all for not. She would need all of those well-embedded traits and more to raise her own children. As a young mother she called on all the powers within.

Please police, she silently pleaded, *why can't you get him? Come on get it together. I have already told you what you are looking for once. Please don't make me do this again. It's just not my job, damn it*!

Drägo officially dropped out of sight of the Department of Justice and started a new slate of the same material under his newfound identity. That wasn't illegal. He had every right to use his proper name. What it proved to be was a circumstance of enormous convenience. Sandra watched in desperation of how it was used to evade the law even further. She realized why knowledge from his mother about an unknown identity excited Drägo and why he worked feverishly to accomplish it.

Sandra thought about the time the police had locked up his car after ransacking it. They and Drägo were very slack in that case because there were still old ID papers in the glove compartment of the vehicle. The papers or at least the name on them went by unnoticed.

With Drägo's newfound identity life became a blur of antics aimed at out smarting the law and Sandra. He was playing a role and having a riot doing it. The name of the game was "Catch me if you can!"

For six months, Drägo claimed to be working at a large construction project that kept him away from home all week. He claimed he stayed "in camp." When Sandra complained about that Drägo said he had no choice, it came with the job. He in fact never was working on the construction site, but always managed to produce money that supposedly came from a paycheck.

Sandra played stupid for a while, but eventually asked him why there was never any sign of a pay stub or anything that would indicate a paycheck. Drägo claimed he left the stubs at the bank. Sandra went to the bank and asked if Drägo cashed regular paychecks there. She was told he did not. She dreaded the truth, but the gig was up and Drägo knew it. When confronted by Sandra, he finally admitted he hadn't been working anywhere other than in other people's businesses stealing their hard earned dollars. The information wasn't easily offered. Drägo told her every lie he could muster up to start with. Sandra counter acted him every time he opened his mouth. Sandra wouldn't let up until he told her the truth. The rules of the game had changed. Sandra wondered how Drägo managed to hold up as well as he did under police interrogation.

Finally realizing defeat, he looked at her and shook his head.

"Boy, the guys back in the pen would never believe I am living with someone as straight as you are," he told her as if he himself was amazed.

The truth be known, he was amazed. Sandra never ceased to amaze him. The police never ceased to amaze her.

Members of the city police department began visiting Sandra regularly in the middle of the night always inquiring about Drägo's whereabouts. Sandra thought it was obvious that she knew less than they about that and told them so. They had at least had some recent contact or trace of him however indirect it may have been. He had been caught with a stolen car and used the old line of needing to go to the bathroom. The police fell for it. Drägo escaped on foot. There had been a rash of stolen cars and break and enters the police told Sandra.

Drägo didn't like to use his car when he went out on jobs after the lock down of his own in the alley. Sandra almost sympathized with the police because they were really distraught. Even knowing what they were going through trying to catch the man Sandra couldn't help but get annoyed about being woken in the dead of night. She had to get up for work in the morning.

After three times consecutively Sandra asked in a half-hearted joking manner, "Don't you guys have anything better to do than keep waking me up in the middle of the night?"

One officer apologized and said, " I just got through saying to my partner that I hate to have to wake you up again, but there is another car missing from the same area as last night."

"Well, what do you want me to do about it?" she asked, making no attempt to conceal her frustration.

The other officer developed an attitude.

He was very unprofessional and showed it when he blurted, "You got any bones about us searching this place?"

He was really rude. Rudeness deserves rudeness. Sandra spewed his own tone of voice right back to him. She knew he didn't have a search warrant, but was trying to intimidate her.

She spit back at him, “I have already told you he is not here. You can search all you like, but you won’t find him and don’t you dare wake up my kids in the process!”

Sandra couldn’t be intimidated. The house wasn’t searched. Both cops ended up sympathizing with her because they knew she was in a helluva position, even more so than they. The officer with the attitude apologized to her.

Sandra came close the first evening to spilling her guts to the one officer who wasn’t rude. He had talked to her alone at length the first night. She lied to the officer feigning ignorance of any criminal activities. Mixed emotions ran rampant. He looked at eight by ten pictures of Steve and Susan asking if they were Sandra’s kids. They were beautiful looking little kids he told her and continued to say it was too bad for them to have to live in a criminal life. Sandra didn’t say anything because she was afraid and at the same time in love with the man they pursued. Mention of the kids was an intimidation tactic as well but if there is such a thing as sincere intimidation that was it. Sandra suspected that a partner must have been outside. They thought that two cops questioning her might have been overwhelming. There was a very frustrated police force out there. There was also a very frustrated young mother with two young children caught in the thick of the situation. She wished the police and her could help each other, but she was afraid she would not be protected. She feared their only mission would be to get their man.

During that same period of time, the family’s home was under twenty-four-hour surveillance. The police force never even attempted to be inconspicuous. They sat on the street right outside the front door. Sandra thought that was a stupid move, down right ridiculous. She wasn’t a convict who had ever seen such things before but no one could miss the surveillance.

Drägo knew what he was looking for when he did periodically sneak into the house. Side door. Back window. Anything that didn’t face the front of the house allowed him undetected entry day or night, terrifying Sandra. There were no back alleys in the neighborhood. The back yard of their home was large and fenced by chain link. Back yards of other properties on neighboring streets all met in the middle forming a square. There was nowhere for anyone to park a vehicle unless in someone's back yard. Sandra pondered that. She often watched Drägo mold simple everyday things into something that would be advantageous to his career, including picking a home for his family. His criminal mind never stopped.

Susan was three years old when she saw someone other than Drägo trying to get through a back window of the house. Sandra's cousin was visiting. Drägo wasn't home. During the visit, everyone decided to go for ice cream. When they got back home Sandra realized she had locked them out. She mentioned to her cousin that he could go through the dining room window like Drägo always did. Sandra and the kids waited by the door around the corner of the house. Susan was watching the cousin when she exclaimed to her mother that Uncle Louie, as he was called, was breaking windows. Sandra told her that he was just trying to get in to unlock the door for them. Susan insisted he was breaking windows. Sandra stepped around the corner to see why the three year old was being so persistent.

Louie was a small man. Sandra burst out in laughter when she saw his small butt, short legs and little cowboy boots hanging out of the window. When he tried opening the window after scaling the wall the window had come off of its track and slid inside skidding across the kitchen sink landing on the floor. It must have been a helluva clatter. An older woman who didn't speak English stared in horror at the man coming through the window. She had watched his every move. Sandra stood in the back yard and roared with laughter. While Louie was hanging half way in the window he tried to explain to the woman, who couldn't understand him, that the break in was a mistake. Finally, the woman's son who spoke English entered the kitchen and relieved Louie from his perch at the window of the side-by-side duplex house. Louie had gone one window too far.

The comic relief was short lived. A few days later Sandra's boss gave her a telephone message to pick up Drägo at the train station that night after work. He was coming home by train. She never did ask him where he had come from because she just didn't want to know anymore.

When Sandra arrived at the train station, so did three uniformed police officers. Attempting to determine if their presence was a coincidence or deliberate Sandra stood along side the train track looking up and down it as if she was directionally challenged. The truth is, she was. Regardless, her suspicions were confirmed. A policeman stood within five feet of her. Sandra almost smiled because she was thinking he must be directionally challenged as well because he to looked up and down the empty track.

Not a word was spoken although direct eye contact was made twice between the pair standing at the edge of the empty railroad track. Sandra deliberately looked the officer square in the eye in the hope that he might say something revealing. After all she had already seen a lack of professionalism before that, so she thought why not give it a shot. She even toyed with the idea of asking him if they were waiting for the same person. She was looking for an opening to tell what she did know to the officer. Possibly together they could entrap Drägo, but could she trust him to keep her name or knowledge of any conversation between them off the record. She felt she didn't dare risk it. So no conversation ever took place between the train watchers. Both Sandra and the cop ended up looking like fools looking up and down an empty track.

The first one to make a move was the policeman. He suddenly turned on his heals and entered the train station but stood in full view of Sandra at a large front window. She turned to look directly at him just to let him know that she knew he was still watching her. That was when she noticed two other uniformed cops standing in clear view as well inside the building. Then she started to feel really stupid herself and went and sat in her car waiting for the train to arrive. The train arrived. Many passengers disembarked. The train left. There was no sign of Drägo. Sandra sat in her car at the station for probably half an hour after the train left.

Now what? She silently mulled over the situation.

The police stayed as well. It didn't matter what she decided to do. She guessed the police would do the same.

Sandra decided to check out the situation. Leave the train station. She couldn't camp there anyway. She had to pick up her children at the baby-sitter's. The unexpected trip which was all for not and the untimely delay waiting for a passenger who never appeared had her running far behind schedule. Sandra did have the forethought to call the baby-sitter from work and say that she would be a little late but by then she was really late. The police had gone and sat in their vehicles as she had. Sandra made the first move. It seemed to be her turn.

"Ok boys, let's go," she mumbled aloud, while she put her car in gear.

The officer who accompanied her at the track was the first to move in behind her vehicle as it left the parking lot and motored into the lanes of the main street of the city. The other two followed suit. All three police vehicles were ghost cars. The blue uniforms blew their covers, but not their intent.

Stupid, stupid, stupid, Sandra thought shaking her head.

Sandra drove like she had seen Drägo drive many times looking as much into the rear view mirror as looking ahead. The first car to leave the train station behind her followed her for half of the trip to pick up her children. Becoming too obvious another car picked up her tail. She wanted to check out if that was what had really happened so she stopped at a coffee and donut shop along her route. Sure enough the car in her rear view mirror pulled into the parking lot behind her. She knew how much police like coffee and donuts.

Sandra sat on a stool at the counter and so did the police officer, two stools from her. Direct eye contact was made, but no words were spoken. Again, Sandra entertained the idea of talking to the police but she didn't have time for any long tales. She had to pick up her kids. She abruptly got up to leave after finishing half a cup of coffee. The police officer left as well, right behind her. Sandra held the door for him rather than letting it slam behind her while they both exited the building. Each of them knew what the other was doing. Within a couple of blocks, Sandra noticed the third vehicle from the train station behind her. Her coffee buddy had backed off. Their ghost cars were not very ghostly. Ghost cars with uniforms inside already identified. Get a real job! A patrol car would have been less obvious because they were everywhere all the time anyway and cops all look the same in their uniforms.

That was the day when Sandra realized she was being followed everywhere because no one had any way of knowing that she was to meet Drägo at the train station. She had her suspicions of being tailed before that, but thought she was being paranoid. The incredulity of life with Drägo sunk in to the core. She gave up watching for tail gaiters. She just didn't care anymore. She knew the law was following her with the hope of finding Drägo. The police didn't know just how cunning he was. Evidently neither did Sandra.

After collecting her children from their baby-sitter's, Sandra went directly home. She was numb. Drägo couldn't come home. A look out the living room window revealed a different ghost car sitting directly across the street from her home. As much as she had secretly wanted him to get caught, the thought of Drägo never coming home again made her very sad. She kept telling herself that she had wanted that for a long time by then. Still she couldn't help but wonder how she was going to explain Daddy's absence to her young children. They loved him and so did Sandra. She tried consoling herself. The life they led because of his activities couldn't go on much longer anyway. She wouldn't raise the children that way.

A little shuffling sound. Another. Sandra's mind was forced back from worrying about the future to the present. Someone was sneaking up on her. She shot a terrified glance in the direction of the noise. Drägo!! She stood in the middle of the kitchen watching him come through the dining room window on the back wall of the house.

"My gawd, where the hell were you?" she almost shouted at him, "I was at the train station and so were three cops!"

"I know you were there. I saw you and I saw the cops to," he told her.

"Well where did you go? How come nobody saw you?" she asked still stunned by his presence. She had been home for about an hour.

"When I saw you and the cops I knew you had been followed. All the passengers got off one side of the train. I got off the other side," he said with his usual smug look.

Sandra told him about being followed home and the fact that there was surveillance sitting across the street from their home.

"Why do you think I came in through the window?" he asked her, "The door would have been a helluva lot easier. Don't you think I would have used it if I could have?"

Sandra stood there shaking her head in disbelief looking at the man she loved wondering what she was going to do with him or worse yet, about him.

After three weeks of their home being under constant surveillance, Sandra talked Drägo into turning himself in for whatever it was the law wanted him for. Many tears later from both of them they walked into the city police station. They asked why their home was under surveillance, why police officers kept waking Sandra up in the middle of the night. Just what did they want?

Sandra remembers the episode well. The Sergeant behind the front desk looked at her as if she wasn't operating with all of her faculties after she explained everything that had transpired over the past three weeks. Sandra finally did manage to convince him that she wasn't an idiot plying for attention after he suggested that just possibly someone could be pulling a prank with the invasions.

"This is no prank," Sandra responded in frustration, "unless someone is stealing uniforms and patrol cars from the police department! Have you had any reports of that lately?"

The sergeant couldn't say there were any such reports. Sandra knew that but was making a point as usual. The nighttime visitors always arrived in a patrol car and wore uniforms. The cop checked his computer and said nothing came up on Drägo's name. That was no surprise to Sandra or Drägo because of the name. After that Sandra was steered into the squad room in the hope the officers she had encountered would be present and she could identify them. The cop who had been rude had red hair. Other than that everyone would look the same in their uniforms. Of course, the red head wasn't on shift. Thirty others were. She couldn't believe what was happening. The smirk on the Sergeant's face made it clear that she was being laughed at. The Sergeant claimed to have no knowledge of the nightmare she was living. Sandra looked like a fool, but she knew who the fools were. Both Drägo and Sandra smirked at the Sergeant for different reasons and then left the building.

The surveillance appeared to stop. There were no more nighttime chats either. That left Drägo free to come and go and carry on his usual antics as he pleased again. He thought it was quite a joke that the police had nothing on him. He got even cockier. Sandra would wake up two or three times a week alone. Drägo was blazing a bolder trail. No one was able to put out the fire.

Drägo wasn't the only one free to go. Sandra packed up the children and left one day when Drägo was not home. It was inevitable that he would be taken away from them. If the police force wasn't going to do it soon, then Sandra had to be the one to make the move. The police had proven they couldn't do it. Sandra wasn't going to sit back and wait for them to get their act together. She didn't want to see it and she certainly didn't want to subject her children to that scene either. One day Daddy would go out to play with his friends and not "be back soon."

Drägo pleaded for his family to go back to him. Sandra refused. It tore her heart out to do that.

Soon after she left Drägo, Sandra realized she was pregnant. Sandra was twenty-one years old with two children and no father. She had an abortion. She still wonders what kind of human being that child would have been. It's like there is someone missing that she never knew. She would not put another child through an uncertain future. Sandra felt she couldn't provide a decent lifestyle for any more than two children. She remembered the poverty of her own childhood at her grandmother's. It wasn't much better at her father's. She didn't want to see a repeat of that for her kids.

Sandra and the children moved to the east coast of the country within a short time of being on their own. That move shook both Drägo and the police. The home base was gone. When the authorities couldn't find Sandra, they started inquiring amongst her relatives as to her whereabouts. They were still trying to keep track of her because losing her meant losing Drägo. Sandra's aunt informed the detectives who visited her that Sandra had taken the children and moved to the coast.

"That's probably the smartest thing she has ever done," a detective told her.

They told Sandra's aunt the whole sordid story of how they had been watching Drägo for years, but had never been able to put anything together because he was so slippery. They admitted that they were baffled as to why there was no criminal record on Drägo because he was obviously a professional.

The aunt didn't put the connection together either of his childhood name or she would have told them. On an occasion after that, she turned him in when he went to her mother's house inquiring about Sandra's new address. When confronted by the police, he managed to slip away that time as well. He slid to the east coast because Sandra's grandfather had said where she was. Her grandfather had always liked Drägo and felt sorry for his quest for his family. The grandfather apologized to Sandra much later saying he hadn't been aware of the harm.

Sandra was never found even though Drägo made two trips trying to locate her. People often miss the obvious. Sandra was listed with the telephone company. Actually, she was listed under Drägo's last name which she had been using since Steve was born. All Drägo would have had to do was dial directory information.

Much later Sandra learned that Drägo had stayed in the hotel right across the street from where she worked. She was right under his nose. Not even someone who repeatedly outsmarted the law thought to look under his own nose. Many people look past their noses, but forget to look under them.

If Drägo had found the children and Sandra at that time he may have found them crying. They cried together. The man they loved and knew as Daddy was gone, but it was a sacrifice they had to make. The children were getting old enough to start understanding or at least ask questions when the police kept arriving on the doorstep. As they got older they would know that the police were not Daddy's friends. Sandra couldn't bear for them to come to the realization that their father was a criminal. In the minds of children the police would have eventually been blamed for his absence. Sandra chose to take the blame, if it ever came to that. Fortunately, it never did. Everyone just cried a lot. They all wanted to go home and they all missed Drägo. Sandra knew they couldn't go home as long as Drägo continued to evade the law.

The family stayed with Sandra's aunt and uncle temporarily. Their house was over crowed with an extra family living in it. Sandra soon got a job in a factory that made submarine detectors. It was tedious work on an assembly line. She wouldn't get a paycheck for three weeks, but even then it would only be for a few days pay. She had found and paid the rent on a one-bedroom apartment, but there was no money left for food. Three weeks was a long time to not be able to feed her kids.

Sandra took time off from her job and went to the local welfare office asking for assistance until she got paid. She hated taking time off from her new job, but she had no choice. She needed to get help. What a farce she was put through at the welfare office.

Sandra sat in the waiting area for a long time, at least a couple of hours. Finally her name was called and she went into an office where there were two social workers, a man and a woman. She tried explaining her situation without revealing too much of her past. The social workers were not happy with her explanation of why she was there and pressed her for more information. They wanted to know how it happened that a twenty-one year old mother of two had moved half way across the country without a father. Chauvinists!

Sandra was reluctant to tell her story, but it didn't look like she was going to have a choice. She told them the whole story of why she felt she had to move her children away from the criminal life with their father and her fear of more physical abuse to her kids. She also told them that she had lived under constant police surveillance because of Drägo. The story sounded so fantastic to the social workers that they asked if Sandra would swear to it on a Bible. Sandra agreed. She knew how her story must have sounded to the strangers. They encouraged her to tell them more every time she stopped talking. She hoped that telling her story might persuade them to help her. They certainly showed interest in hearing it.

Situations that Sandra described just didn't happen to people. Both social workers were smirking at each other as Sandra swore on the Bible vowing her story was true. Sandra was humiliated, but undaunted. She had scraped a bit of food together at home with the help of her aunt. After the humiliation of having to swear that she wasn't a liar she could still see that no one in the office had any intentions of helping her. They suggested she go back to where she came from. She told them she didn't have any money to go back even if she wanted to and that if she had any money she wouldn't be sitting in their office. With that information they told her that they didn't see any reason why their office should help her because it had been her own choice to move her family, regardless of the circumstances. Those circumstances were not their problem she was informed. They also told her that she had a job so she couldn't expect to get any help from the welfare office. They only helped people who were unemployed they said. Sandra thought that was absolutely ridiculous. Helping her was only to be a one-time thing.

"If I have to come in here again I could end up unemployed because I will be fired for taking too much time off work," she told them. "Is that what I should do? Maybe then you will help me."

"That will be your choice," the woman said to her with a nasty attitude and the sneer to go with it.

Sandra found that attitude to be incredible. She could hardly believe what she was hearing. Cripes, all she was asking for was some money for groceries to feed her kids. What the hell was their problem? The meeting ended.

Sandra returned to the welfare office two days later. Of course she had to take more time off work. She was left to sit in the waiting area for about two hours again. She became furious, but contained herself. She inquired at the reception desk as to how long it would be before she would be seen by someone. The receptionist told her that she didn't know and that she should just wait until it was her turn. Many people had come and gone while Sandra had been waiting. Both of the social workers she had spoke to before saw her sitting there and ignored her.

Her turn, she thought.

Just when was it going to be her turn? She told the receptionist that she would be back the following day. Her announcement would be relayed to those who had ignored her. She was certain of that.

The woman's demeanor was that of, *ya, so what? Tell someone who cares.*

Sandra left the building silently vowing, you people damn well will care.

Sandra does not know why she didn't get fired from her job because as promised she was at the welfare office again the next day. It was her third trip. She would not be put off again. She had become a familiar face by then although there was a difference that day. She had both kids with her.

Sandra went to the reception desk to make her presence known, as if she had to. It was just the thing to do. She said she wanted to see the social workers she had seen before. The snooty receptionist told her she would have to make an appointment and then dropped her head back to the paperwork in front of her dismissing Sandra. Sandra became livid. People were walking on her fighting side.

"You go to one of those offices behind you and get someone out here to see me!" Sandra was shouting and making a scene. "Otherwise my kids and I will become permanent fixtures here. Are you going to feed us while we wait?" she asked, glaring at the woman. "We are not budging from here until we get some help!"

Everyone was staring at her. Sandra didn't give a damn. Social workers came out of their offices to see what the ruckus was. Having made her point, Sandra quietly sat down beside her kids. The defiant look on her face told everyone that she meant exactly what she said. She was finished screwing around with them.

The receptionist disappeared from Sandra's icy glare. She went into an office behind her desk. In a matter of minutes both social workers Sandra had already seen ushered her and the kids into an office.

"You've made quite a scene out there," the man said to her with a hint of a smirk.

"I know I did, but that seems to be the only way I can get anyone's attention around here," she said to him. "This is the third time I have been here now and I mean it when I say I will not leave again until I get some help."

The woman spoke up then saying, "We have a suggestion that will probably help you."

"What is that?" Sandra asked, noting the superior look and the familiar sneer on the woman's face.

"We will take your kids and look after them for you until you get on your feet a little better," she smirked at Sandra.

Sandra lost it. She jumped out of her chair and lurched toward the desk the pair was sitting behind. Her action scared her kids. They knew anything could happen next. They hadn't seen their mother angry often, but they knew it was bad news for anyone involved when it did happen.

Sandra placed both of her hands on the desk leaning toward the two social workers and yelled in their faces, "What is wrong with you people? I'm not one of your local welfare cases that doesn't attempt to work! You wouldn't give one of them the same kind of grief that you have chosen to give me! I don't see any of them swearing on a Bible either! I work to support my family! They don't! And now you sit there suggesting that you take my kids because you won't give me any money to feed them for a couple of weeks! No one is taking my kids anywhere! You know damn well that if I was stupid enough to agree to that I may never get my kids back. Maybe I look like I am an unfit mother to you people because I'm trying to look after my kids! Maybe you've been at your jobs so long that you don't know a decent mother when you see one!"

Sandra remained standing holding her ground waiting for a response. She didn't bother to wipe the spit off of her face. The two social workers sat behind the desk looking at her astonished and speechless. Finally Sandra encouraged them to open their mouths.

She spoke again, "Well, will someone please tell me what the hell is wrong with this picture?"

The man found his voice.

"Have a seat, we'll be right back." he said, getting up and motioning for his co-worker to follow him. The woman didn't say a word. She got up from her chair and followed the man out of the room. She looked relieved for the chance to be able to get out of the office. She never did come back into the room. The fellow returned about ten minutes later with a check in his hands payable to Sandra.

"Here, I hope this will help you," he said with a genuine look of sincerity mixed with shame.

Sandra took the check staring him evenly in the face and said, "I'm sure it will. Goodbye."

Sandra took her children and left the building never to be seen there again.

She continued working at the factory for a while after that. Everything fell into place for her and her children. The kids went to day care, which they really enjoyed and Sandra went to work. She took a different job at an order desk of a vending machine company because she was bored with the tedious menial factory work. The new job didn't pay as well, but she wanted the office experience. It could lead to a better position.

With the smaller income she had to take on a second job to keep up with expenses. She got another job working in a lounge on weekends. The job itself didn't pay much for two nights a weekend, but the tips were fabulous. The manager suggested she work there full time instead of working two jobs. She thanked him, but declined because her kids really liked going to day care and she thought it was good for them because they were learning social skills, not relying heavily on each other as they did at home. Sandra needed the extra income of the part time job mostly to pay for the kid's transportation to and from the day care. She didn't have a car, so the kids went back and forth by taxi. It was too far for Sandra to take them by bus and then get to work herself.

Sandra had instructed the day care attendants to never let the kids go with anyone unless she called the center first. She never knew who might be lurking around. She called a taxi to pick up the kids everyday after she got home from work. Then she would call the day care telling them that a taxi was on its way. One day she phoned for a taxi and forgot to phone the day care. She got a phone call from the dispatch office of the taxi company asking her to please call the day care center because the attendants wouldn't let the driver take her children until she did. She apologized for the oversight and said she would call right away. Sandra couldn't help but smile to herself. Her plan to protect her children in her absence was flawless. Drägo would never have come to her apartment to take them. He would scoop them when Sandra wasn't looking. She could relax.

Sandra was at work one day when her aunt phoned her. Another relative had called the aunt to say that Drägo had been in the area twice looking for Sandra and the kids. Sandra immediately thought of the eerie feeling she had sometimes when she was at work in the lounge. A few times she had found herself watching the front door expecting Drägo to walk in at any second. She often scanned a crowd of people waiting to be seated looking for him in the crowd.

As much as Sandra still loved Drägo, she was horrified by the information from her aunt. She called the police when she got home from work. She told them about Drägo's record and a nation wide warrant that was out for his arrest. She said that he was known to be in the area a couple of times before that looking for her. Sandra wanted to warn the police that he may come back and wanted assurance that she could call them if he did show up. The officer on the phone assured Sandra that she could call them anytime and they would dispatch a car to her address immediately.

Some days after that call, Sandra's manager, from the lounge, was in her apartment. He had given her a ride home from work. They were sitting around talking when someone knocked on the door. It was one of Sandra's neighbors from the small apartment building she lived in. The woman asked if Sandra had company. Sandra thought it was an odd question coming from a neighbor, but she said she did have company and asked if there was a problem.

"The police are searching through his car," the neighbor told Sandra.

Sandra thanked the neighbor and thought, *oh good grief! Now I can't even have company just because I told the cops that Drägo could show up. I wondered if calling them was a good idea. Will this never end?*

Chapter Nine

Many months later with news from relatives that Drägo was incarcerated in a western penitentiary, Sandra and her children were able to come out of hiding. Sandra called her last place of employment where she worked when she had lived with Drägo. She told the manager that she was calling from the east coast and told him that she wanted to go home. She asked if she could get her job back.

A job for Sandra would be a deciding factor in their return. She didn't have much money. Sandra wanted to make sure she didn't have to go through the same bullshit she had gone through with the local welfare department.

The manager was happy to hear from her and said, "Anytime you get your short little butt back here, you have a job."

"Ok, see you as soon as I can afford it," she told him.

The family of three returned home about three months later. By the time Sandra bought train tickets for everyone, she didn't have very much money left. Her final paycheck would be mailed to a relative's address about two weeks later. Funds had to be stretched. She remembers being at a large train station where they had a bit of a lay over in travel during the trip. The place was huge. The kids were hungry, so Sandra finally found a buffet style restaurant where the family might be able to afford to eat. Being a train station or anything else like it, the prices were expensive. Sandra carefully compared prices of different food items and picked out some good solid food for the family. The kids eyed all the deserts and fancy looking things and asked if they could have some of them. Sandra told them she didn't have enough money for those kinds of things. Her and the kids proceeded to the cash register with their food on a tray. While standing in a line up to pay for the meal one of the kids spotted some bananas in a basket on the counter. They both wanted one. Again, Sandra said she didn't have enough money for bananas. She tried to say it quietly, but the kids were hungry and tried persisting. An older man standing in the line up heard the conversation. Actually, everyone did. The man told Sandra to let the kids have a banana and he would pay for their entire meal. Sandra refused his offer.

He almost pleaded, "Let me do it for the kids."

Sandra still refused while trying to be polite. The man became persistent. Of course the kids heard the conversation as everyone else in the line up did. They wanted Sandra to let the man pay for their bananas and whatever else. Their mother must have appeared cruel when she not so politely told the man to back off. He persisted. Others in the line up were getting uncomfortable just hearing what was going on. Finally, Sandra looked pleadingly at the male cashier who was slightly older than her. Somebody had to take control. The kids really wanted those bananas by that time and Sandra was in such a position with ten people listening that she just couldn't get the point across as to why they couldn't have them. The cashier saw the pleading in Sandra's eyes and told the man point blank to leave her alone.

"I have heard the lady tell you twice that she does not want you paying for her food, so stop persisting or I will have to call a security guard," the cashier said.

Sandra looked at him embarrassed and very quietly said, "Thank you."

Nothing more was said about bananas by anyone.

After a short stint with a relative, Sandra and the kids moved into an apartment. When the family left the area to go to the east coast, they had left almost everything they owned with the woman Sandra had given the red velvet drapes to. The same woman whose husband could barely support his family of five kids was given a fridge, stove, two new single beds and many other extras that Sandra didn't feel she would need or have room for in an apartment. After she left Drägo, he told her to take the furniture and household things out of the house or it would all be left behind because he would not be living in the house any longer.

Drägo said, "Get it all out tomorrow or it will be too late."

Everything was either stored or in use at the other family's home. At one point Sandra wrote a letter from the coast to the woman saying she would be having her things picked up by a railroad company that would ship it all to her. The woman wrote back and told Sandra that she had moved and wouldn't be giving Sandra's belongings back.

The last line of the letter said, "Don't try to locate us because no one knows where we live."

When Sandra and the kids moved back to the area and found an apartment, her uncle went to retrieve their belongings for them. He told Sandra not to go anywhere near the home. She didn't.

The basic furniture was all she got back. Well, not even that really. There were no beds retrieved. There were no kid's clothes, toys, Sandra's clothes or any other personal affects retrieved. Sandra's clothes fit the oldest daughter in the home. The kid's clothes fit the other four kids. The woman kept a brand new washing machine that she had been using for fourteen dollars that Sandra owed her. Sandra had completely forgotten about the money, but there was no chance to repay the woman either. She wanted the washing machine and wouldn't accept any money from Sandra's uncle who tried to pay her the fourteen dollars. What furniture they did get back was basically ruined. The woman kept their large floor model TV as well. The woman got it all including the kid's baby mementos, photos, Sandra's baby book and a piggy bank with her name painted on it that her mother had bought her when she was a baby. The personal affects meant nothing to anyone other than Sandra and her kids.

The family moved into their new home with what belongings they had left. It wasn't long before Sandra's soft spot for Drägo got the better of her. She felt sorry for him sitting in prison and wrote him a letter. She wanted to let him know that she still loved him, regardless of the circumstances. Over the next year she wrote every week. There was a small grocery store next door to her apartment building with a post office in it. The proprietor used to laugh at her mailing those letters because they would only fit unfolded into eight by ten brown envelopes.

"Looks like these are quite the letters you write," he said to her one day with a grin.

He couldn't miss that they were addressed to a penitentiary.

"Yes, they are," she offered with a faint smile.

Many letters later, Sandra became convinced that Drägo had realized his mistakes. Not having his family and doing time in prison seemed to have hit home with him. Sandra and the children were on the road again. That time they were headed further west to set up residence near the penitentiary he worked in as Sandra had explained it to her children.

Upon arriving inside the prison, four-year-old Steve exclaimed, "Mom, we're in a jail!"

He was ready to take flight at the sight of the guard's massive ring of keys opening the door to the visiting area. His mother took the fright out of his eyes by telling him the old stand-by lie. She thinks that was the only "untruth" she prefers to call it, that she ever told her children. After all, Daddy did work there and he did have to stay there.

Time passed slowly. Something Sandra couldn't immediately determine started nagging at her consciousness during and after each visit to the penitentiary. She heard many stories from Drägo about all the inmates who were there because of some slight misdemeanor the law had apparently blown out of proportion. She listened to stories about others who were heroes at their variety of chosen illegal trades. There were always those who were victims of society as well. Her heart sank further with each tale she was told. Sandra realized she wasn't looking at a reformed criminal. She was looking at someone who had been within the system long enough to believe everything he expected her to believe. To listen to Drägo ninety percent of the prison population were martyrs deserving of sympathy or at the least they were heroes. Sandra began to wonder what kind of fool she appeared to be that she should be expected to agree. She had moved her family three thousand miles for that. She nodded her head a lot. Drägo thought it was in agreement with him. Actually Sandra was trying to keep all her marbles in order, so she would be able to decipher what life was to come to.

After visiting Drägo one day Sandra threw her head into her hands when she got home and whined out loud, "My gawd, what have I done?"

She realized that Drägo's letters claiming reform were what he often referred to later as, looking good on a resume. He spoke that way about anything he endeavored in prison. He knew that staff read all letters to and from the prison.

Drägo's world wasn't the world Sandra wanted for her children or herself, tramping in and out of a prison visiting room. They had to make another life, again. Visits became fewer and further between weaning themselves from Drägo once more.

Chapter Ten

"On the Road Again" became Susan and Steve's theme song. They were highway bound for the west coast leaving Drägo to believe whatever he chose. Sandra sometimes said the kids should have been teaching the geography class in school by the time they entered grade five. People thought Sandra was making a joke. It really wasn't meant to be funny. It was sad. When Sandra heard that Drägo was in jail again, they moved back to the small town they called home. Everyone wanted to go home. There was no attempt made to contact Drägo even though he wasn't far away again in the same penitentiary.

All relatives to the family lived many miles away. As Sandra had explained to her daughter they had left the relatives behind. Sandra had little contact with them. She had just enough contact because of her aging grandfather that a couple of them had been sworn to secrecy and knew how to reach her in the event of sickness or death. That was enough.

Drägo was released from prison after a lengthy stay and traveled fifteen hundred miles to Sandra's relatives to get the make on her whereabouts. The last place he knew them to be living was on the west coast. He wasn't about to scour the west as he had scoured the east. Another aunt of Sandra's told him exactly where her and the children were living. She didn't know it was a secret. Drägo traveled all that distance only to find out that his family was right back where he had last seen them, seventy miles from the gated community that held him for years.

The aunt who had reported Drägo being at her mother's gave Sandra a heads up. Drägo was hot on their trail. That scared Sandra because he hadn't had any contact with them in several years. She was afraid of surprises for her son in the schoolyard of the small town. Steve was thirteen years old. She never forgot the threat that her son could disappear. She didn't know what to expect of Drägo especially when it appeared that she was trying to hide his son from him. That was exactly what she was doing in a subtle way. He couldn't be given reason to suspect anything like it or her son would surely disappear.

Sandra had to think fast. Drägo was only twenty-four hours away or sooner depending on his method of travel. She would not run again. Her children finally had some roots under them. At the same time, she couldn't risk losing her son. What to do? There was only one thing to do. She had to divert Drägo's possible thinking. She called his mother where she was sure to find him unless he was already on the highway. Her quick thinking paid off. One phone call and Drägo was on her doorstep twenty-four hours later. Oh joy, a family reunion, just what everyone needed!

Yes, close call and probably one of the smartest calls I've ever made in my life, Sandra thought when she opened the door to find Drägo standing there. Just hug and smile a lot so as not to arouse any suspicion of anything you have been thinking, past or present.

Hugs, kisses and tears flowed freely among the family of four. All were sincere even from Sandra. She still loved him. She couldn't deny that. The circumstances of life with him were a prime example of the fact that love is not always enough. She loved her children more than anyone and would do whatever it took within legal limits to protect them. Sandra only wanted them to have a normal life. She had tried as best as she knew how and as best as circumstances would allow to give them that. Now Daddy was back and on the loose after a several year reprieve. That put normal in the toilet.

Whatever is to come of us? Sandra worried.

She thought of a line in a song John Lennon sang, "Life is what happens when you're making plans."

Drägo set up house in the rural area close to the small town where Sandra and the kids lived. He got a job to make things look normal. When the police discovered that he was in the area, they stopped him for a supposed routine traffic check. They said they didn't want him living in the area and wanted to know what he was doing there. He said he had a son in the area and could live wherever he pleased. That was a true story. After asking whom his son was, the police warned Drägo that they would be watching him. There was nothing they could do about his presence except brace for the ride that would rock their careers. They patrolled the town and large vicinity surrounding it.

At the same time, Sandra had a warning of her own to give Drägo.

"Don't do anything here in Sticksville (not real of course) because the kids and I have established lives here. It's a small town; the kids go to school here and have many friends. We have lived too many places and have finally planted roots. I promised the kids when we moved back here that they will graduate from school here, if they choose to. Don't do anything that would embarrass them or me," she told him.

Drägo was surprised by Sandra's directness regarding his career. He seemed to Sandra to have been offended by it as well. She almost felt sorry that she had said anything, but she had to protect her children. He agreed not to pull off any criminal activities in the town. He never did.

As in any small community there's always a small crime rate. The police went to Drägo questioning him about every misdemeanor that took place. He just laughed at them. It really was quite ridiculous that they should question him about the petty things that were happening. He wasn't into petty theft and the like. The police knew that from his record. They finally stopped going to him about the petty stuff after he made it perfectly clear to them that small time stuff wasn't his thing and they were barking up the wrong tree.

He asked them, "Would you shit on your backdoor step?"

The officers walked away disgusted but they knew he had spoken the truth. They wanted to pin something on him before all hell broke loose. If they hadn't known before they certainly knew then that they couldn't intimidate Drägo. He was there for the long haul, or however long it took to stop him, whichever came first. It wasn't good news for the police. They absolutely didn't want him in their jurisdiction and were grasping at straws for any reason to rid the area of him. Sandra hoped they could pull it off although she knew that things would get very serious before that ever happened. She didn't hold much hope of a speedy resolution. In the meantime, Steve would get very attached to his father.

Sandra and the kids carried on with their lives in spite of the surveillance they lived under again. Fortunately the kids were not aware of much of it. Drägo was in constant contact with the family although he did start forming a life of his own within the small town. He made friends easily. Women thought that he was an Adonis. It wasn't long before he started dating a woman who owned a local business. He brought her to Sandra's house a few times. The two women tolerated each other, but both knew that they only did that for Drägo's sake. Sandra invited Drägo and his new woman for Christmas dinner. Her name was Denise. Dinner was pleasant.

A week or so after Christmas, Sandra noticed that Drägo hadn't been around for a while. Steve asked her if she had seen his dad lately. She admitted she hadn't. She had failed to mention it because she was concerned about why he hadn't been around. Sandra and Steve both thought he might be in jail. Sandra called Denise and asked if she knew where Drägo was. Denise told her that he was out of town and had called her just the day before.

"Oh, ya," was all that Sandra said.

"Yep, I put him on a train to go to his mother's, but he fell asleep and woke up in the wrong place," Denise told her with a half-assed chuckle.

"Hmm, that's interesting," said Sandra.

Denise told her where Drägo said he was. Sandra didn't bother to ask Denise if she was aware of the fact that he was on the wrong side of the continent to be anywhere near his mother's house. She also failed to mention that Drägo would never reveal his location over the telephone. He was too aware of telephone taps. Sandra guessed that Denise believed what Drägo had told her. She wasn't going to be the one to burst her bubble. She would say nothing. Denise would have to learn on her own as Sandra had. Since Denise didn't particularly care for her there was no point in Sandra trying to warn the woman. She was jealous of Sandra because she had Drägo's son and because Sandra even knew Drägo. Sandra would have just looked like a vindictive woman. Anything she said would be repeated to Drägo. She pitied Denise, but there was nothing she could do to help her. Denise would deny she needed any help from Sandra, of all people.

Drägo showed up about a week later. He hadn't gone anywhere near his mother's. He had managed to get himself back and forth across the international border though. Sandra knew that had been accomplished illegally. He had innocently tried crossing the border once before that and was threatened with deportation. Sandra was well aware of the fact that he had evaded the authorities on his little detour.

She shook her head again and thought, *People, people, get it together. How many years will this take this time*?

Meanwhile Drägo was ravaging businesses in the surrounding territory. The next thing Sandra knew he was dating another woman.

She mused, *Hmm, maybe Denise wasn't as clueless as I thought. Good for her*.

Bonnie was the woman's name. Sandra and her kids knew Bonnie and her kids well. To no surprise to Sandra, Bonnie developed a superior attitude toward her. It was really ridiculous because Bonnie was in fact jealous of Sandra, as Denise had been. Bonnie didn't like the fact that Sandra had Drägo's son either or that she even knew Drägo as far as that goes.

Sandra sat back and said nothing. She carried on with her own life. She felt sorry for Bonnie too, but as usual there was no point.

Drägo called one night and said that he was on the other side of the international border. He talked to Sandra, Steve, Susan and then Sandra again. In total they were on the phone about twenty-five to thirty minutes. He told them he would be back soon. He got back all right, but not before the police cornered him and told him never to return to their country again. After he hung up the phone, he went into a washroom at the gas station from where he had made the call. When he came out there were two police officers waiting for him who called him by name. Drägo questioned Sandra when he got home and asked if she had told the police where he was. She asked how she could have done that because she didn't know.

"Across the border isn't much of a hint," she told him.

Drägo agreed. They both knew then that her phone was tapped. The police had traced the call to a phone booth... somewhere across the international border.

A few months after Drägo's trip, Bonnie called Sandra one night crying. She told Sandra that the police had picked up Drägo. Sandra was alarmed, not for Drägo, but for Bonnie and Steve who liked his dad being around. The boy wished with all of his heart, as Sandra had, that Drägo would put his expertise to rest. Bonnie asked Sandra to come to her house because she needed someone to talk to. Sandra promised she would be right there and hung up the phone. She felt terribly sorry for Bonnie because she knew what the woman was going through. Sandra was at Bonnie's house within ten minutes.

Bonnie looked like she had been crying for hours. She thanked Sandra for coming. Bonnie told her what had transpired that afternoon. She had been with Drägo in his truck. They had driven to another town not far away. Drägo had gone into the only store in the area. Bonnie stayed in the truck with Drägo's dog. All of a sudden the police came skidding onto the parking lot. They grabbed Drägo who had just walked out of the store. He was taken away in the patrol car. Bonnie was left sitting in the parking lot with the dog. She had never had a driver's license. She didn't mention how she had got home, but Sandra knew that Bonnie had friends in the same area where Drägo was picked up so it wasn't important.

The two women sat talking for quite some time. Sandra did most of the talking. Bonnie listened. Sandra told her that Drägo would probably be back although he probably wouldn't have any shoes on. Sandra explained the fancy the cops always took to Drägo's shoes. Bonnie laughed. Sandra continued talking telling her about some of Drägo's many escapades. She tried to keep the stories light, but she didn't veil the truth. Bonnie had stopped crying shortly after Sandra got there. She was soon laughing while Sandra told her about some of Drägo's stunts.

They had talked for a couple of hours when the front door opened.

Drägo stepped into the house. Sandra looked at his feet and then at Bonnie. Both women burst out laughing. Drägo had no shoes on. He was pissed off with their laughter and wanted to know what was so funny. He looked very stressed. He saw no humor whatsoever. He had walked in his stocking feet down a gravel street from the police station to Bonnie's house.

Within a few minutes of Drägo's arrival, Sandra noticed that Bonnie's attitude toward her had changed. It became apparent to Sandra that her presence was no longer required. She left and went home, happy she had been able to console Bonnie.

Drägo went across the street to Bonnie's brother's house to see if he could get a pair of shoes from him. He insisted on trading his half-ton truck for the shoes. He had always been overly generous.

When Sandra asked Drägo weeks later why he would trade his truck for the shoes Drägo said, "Well, he doesn't have any money. I was just trying to help the guy out."

Bonnie and Drägo didn't date for more than a few months after that. Bonnie was crushed. Sandra thought she should have been relieved, but Bonnie was madly in love with Drägo. Sandra knew what that was all about. She also knew that Bonnie was better off without Drägo whether she realized it or not.

Chapter Eleven

Meanwhile Sandra was looking for other living accommodations for the family that had grown to three children. A foster child the same age as Steve and Susan lived with them for two years. She also had to find a truck to move their belongings. Steve suggested his dad's truck. His dad didn't have his truck anymore, but said he could get a friend's five-ton truck to move them. Drägo wanted to know where Sandra and the kids were planning on moving. Sandra had to admit she didn't know at that point. She had been looking for a place without any success.

The family promptly found themselves moved into Drägo's four-bedroom home. He said there was plenty of room for everyone and there was no point in him bumbling around there himself. Everyone would have their own room, Drägo and Sandra included. He was only to be there about two weeks longer. That circumstance was unforeseen at the time, but it came as no surprise because the surveillance was heavy.

Months before the family moved into Drägo's home, two undercover police officers contacted Sandra. She invited them into the house after they said who they were and what they were doing. They had been called in from the headquarters in Riverside because the local police department admitted defeat. They couldn't stop the crime spree that was rampaging through the area, but not in the town itself.

One of the cops wedged his way behind the kitchen table to sit down.

The other went to sit opposite him, but stopped in mid air when Sandra said, "I haven't lived with that man in eleven years. Why is he haunting me now?"

It was a rhetorical question. Sandra was just complaining out loud.

The fellow who stopped in mid air said, "Sandra, you don't have to talk to us if you don't want to, but believe me, he's haunting us too."

They were grasping at straws. Unable to catch Drägo at his unrelenting antics, they were completely baffled. They felt that Sandra was the only one in the area who knew him well. That was correct. Any patterns, quirks, or habits she could tell them about would be of great benefit, she was told. Sandra knew nothing except that his criminal expertise could only be honed as compared to what she had seen many years earlier. Prison is always a learning experience. The officers were not consoled by that information. However, she did mention some of Drägo's past habits that she was sure wouldn't have changed. Drägo was a creature of habit. He was institutionalized from spending many years in prison. The police asked her if he was the type of person to stash money under a mattress.

Sandra laughed at that question. She told them that a mattress had never been his hiding place. Drägo wasn't that conventional. She said they could expect to find money absolutely anywhere. She mentioned the door panels of his car and the flashlight. Sandra held important information that the police had overlooked for years. She didn't mention it that day. She needed time to think about what she should or shouldn't do.

The police knew there were many pieces of the puzzle missing. They hoped Sandra could fill in some of the pieces for them. Sandra thought long and hard for a few days. Morals and emotions battled within. She knew that Drägo had to be stopped. She decided she would release the important information she had. That time they heard what she was saying. She made sure of it. She wasn't going to let it slip by the authority's attention again.

"Have you ever heard of the name Drägo Sloitik?" she asked them point blank.

"Well yes, but that's just one of his many alias's," one of two undercover cops told her, ready to dismiss the information.

"No, it isn't. That was the name he was raised under. Punch that name into your computer and you will see the scroll that comes back to you." Sandra persisted, "That's where you will find the criminal record that no one else has been able to find in the last thirteen years."

The police force should have been embarrassed. Because of a complete lack of communication they simply focused on chasing a man they couldn't really even identify. There was no reason for them to be baffled by his apparent lack of a criminal record. Sandra had told them who they were looking for damn it. They didn't hear her until many years later when she insisted they hear her. After all they were the ones who came asking her for help. She had to make them sit up and pay attention. When they did, they found the golden egg that had eluded themselves and many before them. Sandra admits that the information didn't speed up the process any but at least then the police knew exactly whom they were dealing with.

Eight undercover policemen had been in the town for six months at that point executing the surveillance of one man. They would be there much longer. The two officers who contacted Sandra chose to make their presence known to Drägo hoping to make him nervous. They wanted to see if they could trip him up. The other six stayed undercover.

Sandra thought, *Yep, good luck boys. Let's just see if you can trip him up.*

The pair who surfaced took to following Drägo around in the daylight hours. They sat at his job site while he worked. They sat in plain view a short distance from his trailer when he was at home. If Drägo left to go into town, they went to town as well. If Drägo went for coffee, they went for coffee. If Drägo went for lunch in a restaurant, they went for lunch in the same restaurant.

One particular time when Drägo took Steve for lunch, the police went for lunch as well. Drägo and son were the first to get up to leave. Of course that was the norm. The police never left until Drägo did. He got to the counter to pay for their lunch and the policemen were standing right behind them waiting to pay for their lunch.

Drägo turned around, looked at them and said, "That's ok, boys, I've got it. I make more money than you do."

He paid for all four lunches. They left together and got into their respective vehicles.

One of the cops told Sandra about that episode declaring, "Imagine the audacity of him!"

Nothing Sandra heard about Drägo surprised her. The same cop told her about another stunt Drägo had pulled. The two policemen were at their post outside of Drägo's home. It was a hot muggy day in the middle of summer. The police sat in their old car. They could hardly put the car windows down because every time a vehicle went by them on the gravel road, they would eat its dust. They felt absolutely miserable. They had been sitting at their posts in the heat and dust for weeks.

Finally some action took place. It was three in the afternoon. They both sat up and paid attention. Drägo was coming out of the trailer. He got on his motorcycle. He was driving very slowly directly toward them balancing something on the handlebars of the motorcycle.

"Now what the hell is he doing?" one of the cops asked the other.

"God only knows," answered his partner.

Drägo stopped the motorcycle beside their car and said, "Here boys, it's coffee time. You guys look like you deserve a break today."

He handed them a thermos of coffee and a bag of doughnuts.

On a previous occasion before the two cops made their presence known, Steve was alone at his dad's watching TV one afternoon. Sandra and the kids hadn't moved into Drägo's home yet, but Steve spent a lot of time there. Drägo had gone to town for something. Sometime later the TV started screwing up. It got progressively worse. The picture went to pure snow and the sound was pure static when Drägo pulled into the driveway with his car. The picture and sound returned to normal when Drägo shut the engine off. Steve mentioned it to his dad when he came in.

"Oh, really," Drägo said, "take the car down the road a mile or so and turn around and come back. I want to see this."

Steve did what Drägo said. Seconds after Steve got back into the driveway and shut the car off, Drägo showed up outside. He got down on all fours looking under the car. He jacked the car up because he couldn't see under it well. He found a tracking device on the frame. The car had been in a garage on a hoist for some kind of repair a few days before that.

Within a couple of days the police called Drägo asking for their equipment back. They told him it was an expensive little piece of equipment.

"Well, I dunno. I'll have to see about that," Drägo said without malice.

He called his lawyer and asked what he should do with it. The lawyer told him to do whatever he liked with it, keep it, give it back or whatever. The police would have no recourse with whatever he decided to do. The next day Drägo walked into the police station and went up to the reception counter.

"Here," he genuinely smiled at the receptionist, handing her a plastic sandwich bag. "There's a couple of boys around here looking for this little gadget."

The tracking device was inside the bag smashed into miniscule pieces.

Sandra recalls some of Drägo's other stunts. When the kids were babies, Sandra came across Drägo a few times while she was driving down a city street. He would wave to her from a stranger's car that he had stolen. Sometimes when he stole a car out of a private driveway in the wee hours of the morning, he would return it before the owner got out of bed. It would have never been noticed missing. Drägo himself would give its previous absence away. If it had been a profitable night for him, he left money on the driver's seat to cover the cost of gas. He covered more than the cost of the gas. Drägo always left a one hundred dollar bill. The car owners probably hoped that he would return to borrow their car. Drägo often did return. The result was always the same. He had made some unseen friends.

Sandra wondered if the people had ever watched their own private Robin Hood stealing away in their cars. The incidents were never reported. Who would ever report such a polite, harmless and generous thief?

At that time a bare few of Sandra's relatives were aware that Drägo was a thief. That wasn't because he had ever stolen anything from them. He would give them money rather than take it from them. They knew that. Drägo never stole money or anything else from private homes except cars of course. An uncle of Sandra's was one of the relatives in the know. Drägo told him.

Sandra remembers a particular day when her and Susan were home alone. Susan was a baby crawling on the floor. Sandra was pregnant with Steve. The door to the apartment opened up unexpectedly. Drägo walked in with Sandra's uncle behind him. They were chuckling between themselves. Their entrance startled Sandra because the door had been locked and she hadn't heard the usual rattling of keys. Smiling she asked them what was so funny. Her uncle told her that he didn't believe Drägo when he said he could open a door with a credit card and how easy Drägo proved it was.

"He had a credit card in his hand before we got to the door. He unlocked the door with it and didn't even break stride," the uncle laughed with amazement.

Ya, that's a big joke, Sandra thought as her smile disappeared.

Sandra got her turn to laugh a few days later. Her and Drägo had gone to the garage to pick up their second car that had been in for repairs. When they arrived they didn't see the car on the parking lot. Drägo went inside and didn't see the car. He asked the proprietor where his car was.

"It was stolen last night," the proprietor said, looking rather sheepish.

"Nah, you're pulling my leg," Drägo said chuckling. "Now where's my car?"

"I'm telling you it was stolen off the lot last night. I'm not kidding," the fellow said.

After some more discussion about it the proprietor told Drägo that the police had been contacted so all they could do was wait and hope the car was found in one piece. Drägo went back to the car where Sandra and Susan were waiting for him. He was shaking his head looking angry and stunned all at the same time.

"What's wrong?" Sandra asked him.

"Somebody stole the car last night," he told her, still in disbelief.

"You're kidding!" Sandra said to him.

She really thought he was.

"I thought the owner of the garage was kidding too but he's not. I'm telling you, somebody stole the damn car!" he barked at her.

Sandra couldn't contain herself. She started laughing which made Drägo even angrier.

"What's so funny?" he asked with a scowl.

"Well, don't you find it just a little bit ironic that someone would steal a thief's car?" she asked. "Of all the cars on that lot they had to pick yours."

She kept laughing.

"That's not funny, Sandra," Drägo told her, really pissed off.

"I think it is," she said, "So tell me, how does it feel?"

Drägo didn't answer her. His scowl became more pronounced.

"Now you should know how other people feel when you steal their cars," Sandra couldn't stop smirking at him.

"That's different!" he snapped at her.

"What's so different about it? A car has been stolen. You're just pissed off because you can't believe that someone had the gall to steal yours. How dare they!" she laughed.

Sandra decided it was probably best that she contain her laughter because Drägo was visibly upset. She had made her point. It was all she could do to stifle herself. Neither of them said anything more about it, until they were walking into their apartment. Sandra looked at Drägo and seen that he was still wearing a stunned look. The scowl had disappeared. He still thought it incredible that his own car had been stolen. Sandra couldn't stifle a chuckle when she looked at him

"You really think this is funny don't you?" he asked, looking back at her.

"No I don't," she said suddenly, looking serious.

Drägo looked at her wondering what was coming next.

"I think it's absolutely hysterical!" Sandra burst into uncontrollable laughter. She was soon wiping tears from her eyes.

"Well it's not," he tried saying gruffly, but he burst out laughing himself.

"Ya ok, you're right," he said to Sandra, admitting to the irony of the situation. "I just never thought it would happen to me."

They both laughed.

Chapter Twelve

Sandra had many occasions to speak with the two policemen who had originally sought her out during the small town undercover operation. They really thought she knew something incriminating. Steve was used as a scare tactic. It was suggested to Sandra that Drägo was getting old and may be looking for someone he could teach the tricks of the trade. Her confidence was never understood when she claimed that would never happen. Drägo would not do that to his son or her. She was adamant. Sandra thought she saw slight looks of pity pass between the officers because they were not as confident as she was regarding the matter.

Maybe it wasn't a scare tactic, she thought.

Regardless, Sandra knew Drägo. They didn't. Without hesitation, she told the police they were wrong.

Sandra met the cops on the street one day after she had bought a different car.

"Oh, Sandra, you bought a different car," one of them said to her.

"No, I didn't," she answered. "The bank did," as she motioned with her head toward the bank in view down the street.

The cop looked toward the bank. Nothing more was said.

Sandra knew they didn't believe that she wasn't benefiting from the proceeds of crime in some way or another. She was happy to get the opportunity to point out a bank loan. She knew they would be asking about the car, but she had an excellent paying job with the government long before that.

Before Sandra and the children moved into Drägo's, she called one of the surfaced cops she had talked to and told him they would be living there. She wanted to let him know that if her car disappeared from the driveway in the night it would be Drägo driving it, not her. The policeman was elated that Sandra had moved into Drägo's home. He told her if she could come up with any convicting evidence on Drägo she would be paid enough money to be able to relocate. He tried making it sound like a bonus to her life. Relocate! Isn't that all she needed? Sandra told him she didn't want to relocate. The family had lived from coast to coast as it was. She would not break the promise she had made to her kids.

Within a week of the family moving into Drägo's home, a visitor showed up unannounced. His name was Sam. He had been an inmate with Drägo during the last stint in prison. They had become friends. Drägo was surprised to see him. It seemed to Sandra that Drägo wasn't only surprised, he wasn't particularly happy about Sam's arrival.

Sam hung around for several days. Drägo went to work everyday. One evening Sam starting telling Drägo that he needed a ride to the airport that night. He needed to go home because he had found out that day that he had been accepted for a course he had applied for before he left home. The course was to start the next day. Drägo asked how Sam had found out that information. Sam said he had got a phone call informing him of it. He insisted he had to get home. It was late in the evening already. Drägo told Sam that he wouldn't be giving him a ride that night because he had to get up for work in the morning. Sandra was proud of Drägo for thinking about his job that way. She seldom saw him turn down a request from a friend.

Sam got upset. He kept insisting he had to go right then and there. Sandra and Drägo found Sam's sudden insistence peculiar, but neither said anything. Drägo had been suspicious all along of Sam's presence in his home. Sandra didn't know that, but she became suspicious as well. She had been on holidays from work that week and knew there had been no phone calls for Sam. She had been home all day and answered the phone whenever it rang. Cell phones were not common then.

After much discussion Sandra offered to take Sam to the airport. Drägo was about to get irate, so Sandra feared what might happen next. Sam tried hedging his way around Sandra's suggestion. He didn't want Sandra giving him a ride, but couldn't refuse because he had made such a fuss about having to leave. Sandra and a friend of the family's who was there as well that evening left to take Sam to Riverside a couple of hours away.

When Sandra drove into the city, she drove towards the airport. Sam told her that he didn't need to go to the airport right away. He said he had a hotel room within walking distance of it. He wanted to be taken to that room. Sandra said that she thought he needed to get a flight right away although no time had been mentioned. He told her that his flight was very early in the morning so he had got a room to be close. He said he would need to be up bright and early and didn't want to have to bother anyone to drive him so early.

Sandra asked Sam how he got the room because she was sure he hadn't used the phone at Drägo's house. He said he had the room before he went to visit Drägo. Sandra pondered that. She found it odd that he had a room there and had paid for it while he visited Drägo. He didn't seem to have any money during the time he was at Drägo's.

As instructed, Sandra drove to the hotel. Sam told her and the friend to wait in the car until he got the key for the room. Oddly enough again, the key wasn't in his pocket. Sandra and her friend waited for a few minutes and then Sam came back and asked them to go to his room for a drink. Once inside the room, Sam produced an unopened bottle of whisky. He poured drinks for the three of them while Sandra wondered where the bottle had come from. There was no sign of anyone being in the room, no luggage of any sort. Nothing. The room had not been used at all. She thought better of asking any more questions. Something wasn't right.

The three people sat in the hotel room chatting about nothing in general for a few minutes. Then the conversation took on a whole different flavor. Sam started questioning Sandra about Drägo. Was he still up to his old antics? Did she know anything about what he was doing? How did he manage to elude the police?

Sandra pleaded ignorance to all of the questions. Sam kept prodding her to no avail. Sandra and her friend finished their drinks. Sam offered them another one. Sandra refused reminding him that she had to drive. At the same time she could see that her friend wanted another drink. Sandra told him to go ahead, but she would abstain. She didn't want to appear too hasty to leave.

Sam continued questioning Sandra about Drägo, but his questions became more related to what she thought about Drägo's antics. She told him the truth. She thought it was a damn shame that Drägo insisted on wasting his life as he did because he really was a nice person. Sam agreed. The conversation continued along those lines for a while. Then Sandra suggested to her friend that it was late and they should get back on the road to go home. Sam tried coaxing them to stay. Sandra told him they had to leave because it was a long drive home. They said their goodbyes wishing Sam good luck in his course and left. Sandra would learn months later that the police were in the next room recording everything that was said. They played the audiotape to Drägo much later when he was in custody.

In the two weeks the family lived under the same roof, Drägo's antics seemed to cease. If he had disappeared in the night Sandra wouldn't necessarily have been aware of it. They kept separate beds until one night when they made love as if there would be no tomorrow.

Their conversation and love making was all recorded. Sandra claims the only consolation to her is the fact that the police were not working with video equipment. The entire dwelling was completely wired or "bugged" as it is better known, including the telephone.

When there was conversation the general topic was Sandra telling Drägo just how badly the police wanted him because they had offered her enough money to relocate. Drägo decided to lay low to throw off the surveillance. He claimed he would end his crime spree. Sandra knew the words were spoken strictly for a listener's benefit, but he must have sounded convincing to those who didn't know him when he vowed to put an end to his career.

Alarmed that Drägo might do exactly that before they could arrest him on something, anything, all stops were pulled the next morning. A dozen policemen and two police dogs greeted Steve when he responded to a knock on the door. They were quite taken back when the fifteen-year-old boy insisted they produce a search warrant. He had heard his father make the same demand many times. One was produced for the first time. Much to the annoyance of the police, Steve read the warrant line by line before he would allow them to proceed with the search.

The hunt was on for everything and anything. The entire household was ravaged. It ended up the only thing they could find to hold Drägo on were two marijuana plants outside. That wasn't what they were looking for, but it was good enough for an arrest. They had to have seen the plants before that day because they were forever prowling around the trailer. They were just plainly exhausted and felt they had no allies anymore but each other.

The police would rather have found a stash of thousands of dollars. Since Steve was the only occupant of the home at the time he was ordered to direct the officers to the site where his father was working. The road where Drägo lived was about twelve miles long, so Steve led them in the opposite direction of where he knew his father was working. His father was in fact only working a few miles away from the police raid. The officers eventually found the site where Drägo was working and were not happy with Steve when they found it close to his home. When Steve told Sandra about it later he said he had been practicing mental telepathy, which he never believed in, hoping to reach his dad before anyone else could.

The arrival of the police patrol car on the job site didn't go unnoticed. Drägo went flying toward it at the sight of his son in the back seat.

"Steve, what did you do?" he asked, stunned to see his son in the vehicle.

"Wasn't me, Pop," Steve replied.

Even while asking Steve the question Drägo knew that the farce was over. He was arrested on possession of marijuana. After a lengthy investigation, he was also charged and sentenced to five years in prison on twelve counts of safe cracking. The prosecution wanted him for seventy-three, but could only prove a dozen.

On the day of Drägo's arrest, Sandra had driven his green car to work for some innocent reason. She didn't normally drive his car because of the surveillance, not the color. A pair of undercover cops went to her place of employment mid- afternoon requesting her co-operation in the search of Drägo's vehicle. They needed the keys. Sandra gave them no such thing until she pried the information from one of them as to where her son was. Because they were not local police they couldn't really be sure, not knowing the town well or names of people in it. One of them finally said he thought Steve had been taken to Bonnie's house. That made sense to Sandra. She handed over the car keys only slightly pacified. Steve was all right, but Sandra was still concerned for him because of the ordeal she knew he had faced alone earlier in the day. She was glad he was with Bonnie.

Sandra was angry with the authorities. She had specifically asked one of the surfaced cops, before there was any plan of her family living in the four bedroom home, to let her know if he knew of any planned raids, so she could make sure her son wasn't present at the time. As it ended up Steve was the only one in the dwelling when the crunch came down. Many policemen exerted two and a half years of time in total before they finally got their man.

It was because of the broadcasted conversation between Drägo and Sandra that the law moved in when they did. Sandra and Drägo agreed on those suspicions later. The police were afraid, with good reason to be. Any case they had against Drägo was about to crumble. It was obvious to them that Sandra would be of no help to them anymore. She had betrayed them because she wished with all her heart that Drägo would put an end to his career.

After Drägo's arrest, Sandra and her children carried on about their own business ready to tackle anything thrown in their paths although they were very sad.

Both Sandra and Steve did get a good chuckle in though. They had used Drägo's green car to go to town one day. When they got back home, Sandra instinctively hit the lock on the driver's door before she closed it.

Steve looked alarmed and said, "Oh, don't do that, Mom. There's something wrong with the locks. They don't work. Even Dad can't get in. The last time he locked the car he had to go in through the trunk."

Sandra put the key in the lock unlocking the door.

Steve said, "How did you do that?"
"I guess your dad and I use different tools," Sandra said.
"So, what do you use?" Steve asked.
Sandra's response was, "WD-40."

Sam called about two weeks after the arrest. He asked to speak to Drägo. Sandra thought he sounded nervous as if he already knew that Drägo was in jail. She didn't know yet about the hotel room set up that was meant for Drägo.

"He's not here," she told Sam.

"Oh, do you know when he will be back?" he asked her.

"Not for a long time," Sandra said, "because he is in jail."

"Ah, shit! That's too bad," he said, "but I guess the guy will just never learn."

"I guess not," Sandra said rather curtly.

"So what are you going to do now? Do you plan on staying in the trailer?" he asked her.

"Probably. I haven't really thought about it yet," she told him.

Sandra was soon to discover that her dealings with the police were not over. The undercover cop she had spoken with the most, called her at work the next day. He had in fact been the only one she would talk to after a while because she didn't like his arrogant partner. The partner didn't like her either, so they made a poor team.

Sandra's annoyance with the organization hadn't spent its fury. She was really pissed off at the total disregard of her request involving her son. The purpose of the cop contacting her was to tell her they had to get into the home because there was something in it that belonged to them.

Hmm, this will be why Sam called, she thought when the policeman told her what he needed to do. The bugger could have asked me himself if I was planning on staying in the trailer instead of sneaking around through Sam.

She wasn't impressed. She could play games to. Sandra informed the cop on the telephone that she paid the rent there and could see no reason why they needed to return to the home, saying there was nothing in it that belonged to them.

"Yes, there is something there that is ours," she was told.

"Tell me what you people think you have in the place and I'll let you know if it's there," Sandra ventured.

Sandra heard some muffled words as in a hand over the receiver.

The cop came back on the line only to say, "I'm sorry, I can't divulge that information."

"Well in that case, I can't let you in to retrieve whatever you think you have missing either," she responded.

Sandra reminded the cop of the request she had made to him that she felt had been ignored. He apologized for that informing her that he had no idea the raid was taking place until it was already in progress. He wasn't on shift.

Over the course of two days several telephone discussions took place between Sandra and the policeman. During one of those discussions the cop's supervisor got on the phone to talk to Sandra. He knew from the one side of the conversation that he could hear that his subordinate was getting nowhere. The supervisor was demanding, throwing his authority around. He demanded that Sandra let them into the trailer. Sandra refused. He became angry with her. She didn't care. Sandra told him she wouldn't agree to anything until they told her what they wanted. He would not tell her. She said she wouldn't talk to anyone again except the original policeman who had called her. He was the police ace when dealing with Sandra and they all knew it.

Through the course of the conversation with the supervisor, Sandra got angrier than she already was. She told the supervisor that the police accused Drägo of illegal dealings when they had pulled off some fancy tactics of their own. Her tone was nasty and accusatory. She was really pissed off at him trying to shove his rank down her throat. She knew the police were completely stumped and often threw caution to the wind. Although she really didn't think they had done anything illegal her tone inferred that they had. The supervisor went from angry to infuriated. He lost his cool.

"Don't you get smart with me, you little bitch! We have done nothing illegal!" he yelled into the phone.

Sandra said nothing. She calmly hung up the telephone.

She smirked because she envisioned the supervisor glaring into the dead receiver in his hand yelling to everyone in the room, "She hung up the fuckin' phone on me!"

Steve and his friend Pete will never forget the day that a variety of about twenty police cars descended on Drägo's green car in an amazing show of police presence. Ghost cars to paddy wagons to dog carriers with dogs in them made a convoy following Drägo's car that Pete was driving. The entourage seemed to have come out of nowhere.

"Have you been drinking?" Drägo asked Pete.

"No, I haven't been," Pete said.

"Did you do something wrong?" Drägo asked.

"No, I didn't," Pete answered, visibly shaken by the scene in the rear view mirror."

"Well, then pull over," Drägo said, "let's see what these assholes want."

Drägo did all the talking to the police, almost flipping out on them.

He barked at the first cop he saw asking, "What the hell is this parade all about?"

The policeman hesitated before he spoke saying, "There's a chalk mark on one tire. That probably marks a defect in the tire. We suspect all four tires are defective."

"So, you've called out the entire force over what you suspect is a defect in some tires?" Drägo growled. "If you boys ever get your shit together maybe we'll have this conversation again, but in the meantime we're outta here."

Drägo continued barking telling the cop he just replaced tires on three different vehicles because all twelve tires were flat from the barbed wire that had been embedded at the end of his gravel driveway. No one ever found out what the parade of police hoped to find or what the purpose of the mission was. Steve and Pete had never seen such a huge police presence before and fortunately not since either. Drägo, Steve and Pete went back to the scene later and couldn't find anyplace where the fleet of vehicles could have possibly been hiding in wait. There was absolutely nowhere where that many vehicles could hide.

The original cop who had called Sandra when she was at work asked her what time she normally got home from work. She told him. Not unexpected, Steve told Sandra that somebody had called three times for her before she got home that day. Sandra had deliberately got home late because she was pissed off.

"I think it's the cops, Mom," Steve said.

"Yes, it is the cops, Steve," Sandra said. "They have been calling me at work for two days because they want me to let them in here to take out their bugging equipment. I won't let them in until they admit what it is that they are after. So far they haven't, so they don't get in."

Sandra barely had those words out of her mouth when the phone rang. She answered it. The same policeman was on the line.

"Your people were in here long enough on the day of the arrest," Sandra persisted. "Why didn't they take their bugging equipment out then?"

"It couldn't be taken out then because it was installed by professionals and must be removed by them as well," the cop finally admitted because his supervisor wasn't within earshot.

Sandra must admit she was almost gloating after having forced the information from him. She pushed even further.

"I will be here when the professionals perform their task," Sandra said.

The cop's voice sank. He thought he had made some headway with Sandra. He sounded defeated and very tired.

"They will need an hour and a half in the place, alone," he said, sighing as if he were starting from square one again.

The disappointment drowning his voice was more than Sandra could stand. The farce was over. He had confessed as to what he was after. That was all she had wanted him to do. She agreed to a time and date for the unaccompanied entry telling the cop that she would leave the door unlocked. The relief washed over the telephone line. At that point the man seemed in a hurry to get off the telephone as if he feared Sandra would change her mind. Her son had suffered the brunt of the broken promise. The cop knew that Sandra would never forget that even though it was beyond his control. Contrary to popular belief she didn't enjoy giving him a difficult time because he really was a pleasant fellow. There was another reason for her being obstinate. Sandra had to know for her own peace of mind whether or not the place had been bugged. Her and her family's private lives were involved. Steve and her had often reminded each other during conversations that, "the walls have ears."

They often talked directly to possible listeners saying things like, "Ya, ya, we know you're there. How did ya like that one?"

Steve had also picked up a trick from his father. Whenever something of interest about his father absolutely had to be said Steve would motion for silence by raising his hand. Then he would crank the volume of a radio so nothing else would be discernable as they huddled together mumbling what needed to be said.

The family didn't stay long in the trailer after that session with the law. It was too far away from Sandra's job. The kids had a long way to go to school as well. None of them needed to live in the distant boon docks of the locality with winter threatening to howl at the door. Sandra gave notice to the landlord that they would be moving out. They ended up moving out two weeks before they planned to.

Steve still laughs and often tells the story of what became the final flaw in living there. It was fall and some mice had moved in looking for shelter for the winter. Sandra couldn't live with mice in the house. There was nothing in the world that could scare her like one of those tiny little creatures could. Her and the kids walked into the trailer one day after returning from a trip to town. Sandra spotted mouse droppings on the kitchen counter.

"That's it! Pack your bags!" she shrieked,."We're getting to hell out of here, now!"

Both kids looked at her alarmed. Could there be a left over cop somewhere?

"There's mouse shit on the counter!" she said, still shrieking. "Come on, hurry up!"

Within minutes everyone was in the car. No one knew for sure where he or she was going. All they knew was they were definitely going. Sandra was behind the steering wheel driving like a mad woman stickhandling the car in the direction of town. She ignored the snickering she thought she heard coming from the back seat.

Chapter Thirteen

The family unit was split up between two friend's houses for the next couple of weeks. Steve and Drägo's dog stayed with Bonnie. Drägo's dog was a loveable Stafordshire Pit bull. Susan, Sandra and their small dog stayed with a friend of the family's just down the street from Bonnie's house. The small dog was a St. Bernard whose thyroid didn't work so he never grew past the size of a small Springer Spaniel. One day before any of these last episodes started, a policeman asked Sandra what kind of dog it was.

"He's a runt St. Bernard. What other kind of dog would you expect me to have?" she asked, laughing.

The cop laughed realizing she was referring to comparisons often made between dogs and their masters.

Sandra risked going back into the trailer to pack things to move out. She didn't go alone. Steve, Susan and a mini army of movers accompanied her. It was fast.

The local real estate office had a house in the country listed for sale that was also available for rent, since it hadn't sold. It was a three-bedroom bungalow with a basement on ten acres of land with a creek meandering through the property. Perfect! It hadn't sold because of its location. It was located in the boon docks as well in a neighboring rural area, but was only fifteen minutes from where Sandra worked. Another car was required for the kids to get to their school that was fifteen minutes in another direction. The family moved in.

Bonnie and Sandra had a bit of a tussle over custody of Drägo's dog when it was time for the family to move into the rented house. Bonnie thought she could hold onto a piece of Drägo by keeping the dog. The two women were not getting along well because Bonnie was angry at Sandra for living at Drägo's. Steve got along well with Bonnie and besides he was Drägo's son so there was no problem with him staying with her temporarily before a home was acquired. Bonnie was happy to have him and Drägo's dog. If she could have she would have kept both of them with her. Sandra won the custody fight over the dog by telling Bonnie the dog would be better off with her because he would be living in the country. He had lived in the country all his life since Drägo got him as a pup. The dog didn't fair well in town because he wasn't traffic wise. Sandra worried that a car might hit the dog. Drägo had run over him with his car once in his driveway. The dog seemed unscathed by the accident.

Sandra considered buying the house they moved into and began small renovations to suit the family's needs. The basement was soon finished and turned into a family room. The landlord had offered Sandra a rent to own deal with her first year's rent as the down payment. It was a verbal agreement they planned to write up between them. It was a comfortable home and quite spacious. Everyone settled in for a long stay.

The initial year of renting quickly came to a close. With the last holiday of the summer and inevitable winter approaching, Sandra made arrangements with the landlord to install two wood stoves, one in the family room and the other in the living room. She knew from the previous winter that a heating supplement was necessary to keep expenses reasonable. Sandra found wood heat to be very cozy as well. She had deliberately procrastinated on purchasing content insurance until the new system was installed, knowing it would change the transaction considerably.

On a Friday morning Susan and Sandra did their usual thing to prepare for work and school. Steve had also risen from his night time nest to get a ride with his sister into town. He had quit going to school not long after his dad's arrest. His mother was sure he would return to school when he got older. Susan and Sandra rarely saw his face before they left for work and school.

Two vehicles left the driveway that morning, one behind the other,

Sandra in one and her children in the other. Their two pet dogs watched their departure from the yard. Everything was normal.

Sandra had no way of knowing that a few hours later a nearby police station was to receive a small package that contained her intended fate. It was a cassette recording bearing the voice of a man she had previously been dating. His voice stunned the officer listening as it narrated the plan for the day. The narrator was informing his son that he was going to kill Sandra, burn her house and then kill himself. He was apologizing to his son as well for taking the easy way out, as he put it.

Sandra had stopped seeing him when she found him in a compromising situation with a seventeen-year-old girl. In his frustration of being caught, he took Sandra by the throat strangling her. The girl screeched at him to stop. He finally did. From within the labyrinth of his twisted mind he could only see one solution to the rejection he felt when Sandra refused to see him anymore. Sandra had to die. And rather than go to prison, so did he. Even though Sandra had been quite content with single life she had allowed herself to be drawn into the relationship that was short lived.

Sandra will never forget the day she first laid eyes on Larry. He had eyes so brown they appeared black, they transfixed her. There was a striking resemblance to him and an actor with his leathered face that wore the deeply lined features of one who had seen a varied life. Unlike the actor, Larry's face appeared to be split with a permanently fixed white grin. A crown of jet black, almost blue-black, curly hair was peppered with just enough gray at the temples and front to give him a distinguished appearance. Black bushy brows hooded devilish eyes that blinked almost faster than on-lookers could see. His stance was one of complete confidence.

A friend of Sandra's described the relationship between Sandra and the devil-eyed man as a bomb set for detonation. Sandra knew it in her heart as well. She had a terrible habit of ignoring her heart. It was a bad habit she used to batter herself with. It took many years to overcome.

Sandra found herself in the midst of what a card reader described as a torrid affair. She wondered later if the card reader had seen just how torrid things would be in the end. Sandra didn't pay any heed to the warning of her involvement with insanity. She didn't really believe in psychics. Sandra went because a friend asked her to go with her. Sandra looked at it as entertainment.

"There's going to be a sudden death," the psychic told her.

"One of my kids?" Sandra asked in a strained whisper, her voice almost gone.

"No. It is no one in your family. Although it is someone who has been very close to you," the psychic told her, patting her chest in the area of her heart.

"Male or female?" Sandra asked.

"I don't know. The cards don't say. You will have some kind of premonition about it, a dream or something," she told Sandra.

Sandra's first visit to someone in that particular profession pointed out many prophecies. All but one has come to pass. That one may happen after the release of this book. The card reader told Sandra there would be a lot of changes in her life over the next four years.

"Not all of them will be good," she had said with a dire look on her face.

"But you have a knack for being able to set the ship upright after it sinks. You will continue to be able to do that," she assured Sandra.

The woman also said that Sandra had a lethal tongue even though she had barely opened her mouth while she sat listening to the card reader because she was determined not to give the woman any hints about herself. Sandra laughed nervously when the woman talked about her lethal tongue. She decided right then and there that she had better believe everything else the psychic had told her. Sandra had often been told in the heat of an argument that she should have been a lawyer. Drägo was one person who told her that.

Some months later, forgetting about the warning from the card reader of an "involvement with insanity" Sandra started noticing things that made her think Larry could be dangerous. She became frightened of him, but didn't know how to end the relationship. Larry made it clear that there was no such thing as escape. Sandra assumed she had been given the ammunition to end it with reasonable cause when she caught him in the compromising situation. She seized the opportunity to regain her independence and her life, or at least that was her intention.

On the day of the cassette delivery, Sandra wouldn't have gone to work if it hadn't been for her kids. She went to work even though she only had two hours sleep. The evening before consisted of an all night session of arguing and listening to what she thought were idle threats from her would be murderer while he sat in her kitchen. During the arguing, Larry told Sandra that he would burn her house down.

On a previous occasion he had told her, "We're both going to die here, right on the creek bank."

Sandra didn't know that those words were actually a small insight into the thickening plot of her own murder. She took those words to be just a stupid thing that Larry might say in the heat of an argument. When people asked her later why she didn't take him seriously, she told them she had no reason to believe that kind of insanity and asked if they would have. Few asked, but those who did ended up agreeing with Sandra admitting they wouldn't have believed Larry either.

After the all night session, Larry didn't expect Sandra to go to work the following day.

Had it not been for her children prodding her on with, "You should go, Mom. You'll be upset with yourself if you don't," she would have been in the house as Larry expected.

If Steve hadn't surprised his mother and sister with his presence early that morning he would have been killed trying to stop a man who was criminally insane and intent on murder. Someone was looking after the family. It wasn't their turn to be found knocking on Heaven's gate.

At approximately one o'clock in the afternoon, the police station nearest their home received a routine call to attend a house fire. While enroute to the fire, the officer received another call dispatched over police channels from the original department that had received the cassette. The message came from a fear stricken officer telling the other to be on the look out for a black half-ton truck with a lone male driver. He divulged the necessities of the information the cassette contained. Upon arriving at the scene of the fire the officer radioed back to say the black vehicle was at the scene.

There was no sign of life except for one of the pet dogs. It was Drägo's dog. Animal control was called to assist with the pit bull that was near out of his mind from the chaos. His home was on fire and people were flocking from every direction to invade his territory. The scene would have been worse for the dog than the day the trailer was raided. The police told Steve to put the dog in a shed that day or they would shoot it. Old time area residents claimed later they had never seen so much traffic around as the day of the fire and for days later as all the curious came to inspect the damage of the biggest story to hit the rural area in its history.

The cassette recording and the methodologies of the crime proved it was well planned and had been for some time. A wooden sawhorse had been placed under Sandra's bedroom window allowing entry. Gasoline was poured over some laundry in one corner of the basement and lit on fire. The couch in the basement recroom was soaked and lit on fire as well. The main floor was doused throughout continuing down the steps of the front door where it was lit from the outside.

Sandra wondered upon first hearing the story how someone could die in a fire started by his own hand. That wasn't the case. The arsonist's body was found in one of the outbuildings on the property. His head was missing. A shotgun lay on the floor beside his body. He had accomplished most of his mission. He chose the outbuilding instead of the creek bank probably because he would have been breaking his promise to Sandra if he died on the bank alone.

Meanwhile, Sandra's day was zipping along quite nicely, in spite of a lack of sleep, when the company security office called requesting her presence. She was in the security office confronted by the same local policeman who had called her to the security office many months earlier. He had assisted the undercover officers in the search of Drägo's car on the day of the arrest.

"I'm sorry, but we always seem to meet under the most extenuating circumstances," he said to Sandra.

What has happened that this man feels he needs to apologies to me? She wondered. Has something happened to one of my kids? Has Drägo escaped again?

Sandra panicked. News of Drägo escaping would have been a relief. News of losing one of her kids would be more than she could handle. She was speechless. The officer had no trouble finding his voice.

"There has been a fire at your home and everything has been completely destroyed. There is also a man who is deceased," he said.

In the first few minutes of listening to what had taken place at Sandra's home, she was relieved to hear that was all that was wrong. Although she did hope she was having a nightmare from which she would awaken at any minute. She was willing herself to wake up when the realization came that she wouldn't wake up from that one. It was real. Sandra thought she would pass out and wished she could have shut out the voice that insisted on telling her everything she didn't want to hear. The voice seemed to be coming through a small metal funnel. It was mechanical sounding.

The only thought that saved Sandra's sanity at that moment was that her children were still alive. The police officer asked her during the long monologue where her son was. Sandra looked horrified when he asked that question. Did he know something she didn't? Had Steve gone back home with a friend? Sandra told the officer that Steve had left the house with his sister that morning. He was probably at a friend's house in town. She prayed that was true. Sandra found Steve later at the other police station where Drägo had lost his shoes. She had gone to Bonnie's to see if he might be there. Bonnie told her where he was. Sandra thanked God many times for sparing the family from what would have been a merciless, torturous, death. She had no concern for their material lives.

While still sitting in the security office and after establishing that there were no other dead bodies found, Sandra's concern turned to the pets. Were they alive? They were outside when the family left that morning. She thought of the hell they must have witnessed. The officer could only tell her about the Pit Bull and Animal Control being called to contain him. The police had tranquillized the dog before when they had installed the bugging equipment in Drägo's trailer. Over the telephone, the cop inquired as to the whereabouts of the St. Bernard. No one knew where he was. He was eight years old. He had been the family pet since he was a month old. He was one of the few things in their lives they had managed to hold on to over the years.

Sandra's mind's eye flit from face to face of others the tragedy would affect. Larry's son, his estranged wife and Dear Lord, his present girlfriend. Larry had moved in with her after Sandra had stopped seeing him. The woman had attempted suicide once upon learning that Larry and Sandra were dating. She always had a thing for Larry and felt sure that if him and his wife ever separated Larry would turn to her. That didn't happen. Fear wrenched Sandra's heart as she asked the officer if the girl friend had been informed or if they were even aware of the relationship. He said they did have knowledge of the live-in relationship, but that the woman hadn't been told as yet.

Sandra pleaded, "Please make sure the officers who tell her don't leave her alone. Make them aware of the circumstances or there will be another suicide before this is finished."

Another call was made to the police station to relay Sandra's request and the reason for it. The cop assured her that the woman wouldn't be left alone after hearing the news of the tragedy.

Larry left the woman's home that morning armed with a rifle, a large box of wooden matches and two cans of gasoline. Sandra learned that later, plus the fact that the woman had sat with Larry since very early morning talking mainly about suicide and its affect on those left behind. He made his exit packing the artillery when she stepped out briefly to go the store. She never saw him again.

Sandra's heart will forever go out to her. Although, she knew she couldn't help her because she was one of the people who would blame Sandra for Larry's death.

Sandra spoke to one of the members of the local police department a few days after the tragedy. The cop wore a look of compassion on his face when he suggested the children and Sandra go to the house to see what could be salvaged from the one room that hadn't burnt. That was Susan's bedroom. The window was closed because Susan was always concerned that it might rain on her bed. Her ceiling fan was off and the door was closed. Heavy smoke damage was the extent of the destruction. The rest of the house was completely destroyed.

Sandra and her kids stood outside the house dazed looking at their material lives in ruins, still in disbelief of the whole tragedy but thankful to be alive. After a few minutes of looking at the devastation from outside, the children entered the house to go to Susan's room with a reminder from Sandra as to what the police had said. The family had been warned by the police not to go into the kitchen or living room as what remained of the floors were not safe to walk on. The fridge and stove had fallen into the basement when most of the kitchen floor collapsed. Sandra could only force herself to walk in the back door and stand there waiting for Susan and Steve. She surveyed the charred scene, as if she recognized nothing until her eyes fixed on a body on what was left of the kitchen floor. A few seconds passed before she realized what it was. It was the body of their pet St. Bernard. She ran out of the house screaming for the children to get out of the house. Sandra didn't want them to see the body of the beloved pet. They had lost a member of the family.

Afterwards, Sandra had occasion to speak with another officer from the local police department. He was known in the area for his condescending attitude.

"There was fifty dollars in rolled coins in the deceased's truck," he said to Sandra in a snarky authoritarian voice.

"Yes, what about it?" Sandra asked, ready to fight.

"Do you know where it went?" the cop asked her getting more belligerent.

"Yes, I do. My son took it," she told him with an icy glare.

"That's theft!" he said, glaring back at her, "I'm going to have to speak to the prosecutor about this because there may be charges laid."

"Charges? That man took everything we owned and you're talking about laying charges against my son over fifty dollars!" she shouted at him.

"That man, as you call him, lost his life over this," the cop glared back at her.

"That man took his own life and would have taken anyone else's who would have been there!" Sandra spit back at him. "When you are talking to the prosecutor about this make sure to tell him that he will have to lay charges against me to because I agreed that Steve should take it out of the truck, so that makes me an accomplice to any bogus bullshit charge!"

Sandra turned and walked out of the police station. The cop mumbled something behind her that she didn't hear. He was infuriated. So was Sandra. She didn't give a damn what he was saying. She refused to stand there and listen to anymore of his bullshit threats.

No one ever knows how a small town is going to react under dire circumstances. They can be loving and caring or cruel and heartless in the face of disaster. Sandra knew that rumors would be running rampant. When one of her friends tried telling her about some of the rumors, she said she didn't want to hear about them.

The local press tried to get the story from the police hoping to squelch some of the gossip. The police wouldn't give out the information saying that both families involved had been through enough without seeing the whole sordid story in print. A newspaper reporter told Sandra that she had tried to get the story for the sake of the family.

Two or three weeks of ludicrous speculations and out and out untruths surfaced from every corner of the locality. Sandra seldom went out in public but when she did, she had said little to anyone about the bazaar events. Her silence left the grapevine open to all those who chose to punish her for remaining alive after the horror of that fatal day in early September. One old fellow told her that she should have died in that fire. Another fellow looked at Sandra standing in a crowded public place and shrieked to everyone that she had killed a man. The last straw for Sandra was when her friend insisted she listen to one of the rumors. The story was that Larry had found out he had aids and had contracted it from Sandra. That was it.

"You have to say something, Sandra," the friend pleaded with her.

"You're right. Keep your eye on next week's newspaper," she told her friend.

The local newspaper only came out once a week in the small community. Sandra's fighting side rose to the occasion. She knew that what needed to be said had to be voiced by her alone. She wrote a letter to the editor of the small town newspaper. The words had to be chosen carefully. Knowing she would only have, and want, one crack at it, Sandra knew everything had to be spelled out explicitly without risking a lawsuit. The editor/owner of the small newspaper, a man who made his living with words, was reduced to a stutter when he finished reading the article. He sat staring at the pages until Sandra wondered just what he was seeing other than the print. He saw something but sat at his desk speechless.

"So?" she asked, breaking the unnatural silence that had fallen over his office, "Do you think I'm being too rash here or do you think I have got my point across to most people?"

"No, I don't think you're being too rash at all. I certainly think this should straighten out most of them. Of course there will always be one or two that will never be convinced of anything other than the fact that they feel you are responsible for all of this. Most will see the truth with this letter. I appreciate that you gave us a mention because we did try to get the story," the editor said.

"Do you see anything in it that could leave me faced with a law suit?" she asked.

Stuttering again he answered, " I .. I .. don't see anything that jumps off the page and slaps me in the face, although I am going to have to read it again just to be able to digest it all."

"Then print it exactly as it is," Sandra said, "and . . . thank you!"

Sandra appreciated the editor's candor. She left him nodding his head with a look of dismay on his face. As Sandra closed the door to his office, she glanced back at the newspaper editor. He was pouring over the paper in hand again, digesting it. She suspected that he wouldn't be the only person that would read it more than once.

The following is precisely how Sandra wrote it and how it appeared in the newspaper, with one exception—she gave it no title. The editor chose the title without her knowledge and letting her know that he understood.

VICIOUS GOSSIP IS THE ROOT OF ALL EVIL

I don't know who the wise person was who first

spoke the famous words, "Money is the root of all evil." Begging this person's forgiveness I wish to correct him or her because in far too many instances it has been found that vicious gossip is the root of all evil.

In the recent arson/suicide tragedy of which the authorities wouldn't permit a news release, the people who resort to viciousness at other people's expense came out of the woodwork. The press hoped to squelch rumor and gossip by printing a factual account of the incident. The police wouldn't release any information as they felt the two families involved had already been through enough. Both were right.

Unfortunately there are a handful of the narrow minded who choose to blame one particular survivor for another person's insanity. Neither a factual account nor silence would be respected by the handful that has chosen to condone this type of conduct by the criminally insane, as my Doctor referred to him. I feel sorry for the people who are so busy practicing hate stares that those same eyes cannot see past the wall of hatred they have built up. They cannot feel what is humanly expected of them. The son left to mourn. The children left homeless. Those are the people we should be concerned for. Why are we concerning ourselves with trying to add more torture to an already devastating occurrence? Remember I'm only referring to a handful of people. Fortunately, most people can see the tragedy and the loss to both families and can feel the compassion that any decent and sane human being would feel for all the survivors. God forbid this could happen to any one of our number one gossips. They would expect compassion and understanding from the rest of us. I personally would be one of the first to offer what understanding and compassion is needed to repair the damaged souls ripped apart by such a horrendous injustice. This ring of vicious gossip is particularly disturbing because those partaking in this act are not aware of any of the prior threats and physical assaults committed. Even though the criminal in this case had struck up and was cohabiting in another relationship, some people still cannot see beyond the walls of their narrow minds. In these minds the criminal has been turned into a hero in this case of vindictive insanity. As I've already stated, I feel sorry for the people condoning this type of behavior and that feel justice has been done. Those are the people who are capable of inflicting the same kind of pain and suffering on anyone who rejects them. It's a horrifying thought to know that there are others in our town capable of the same form of insanity. I only know that many lives have been devastated by this incident and I pray that the cruelty of it all soon stops to allow the victims and the mourning to continue rebuilding their lives and souls. It is not just to blame one person for another person's insanity. Is there no justice, no compassion, no realization that the full story has never been told and will probably remain untold to protect the memory of the deceased. I am not out to mar this memory for friends and loved ones. I only hope the handful I speak of can give the survivors of this tragedy the same courtesy.

There is no need to sign the name of the person who wrote this. Everyone knows who I am, particularly "the handful."

Forced to sit up and pay attention, most people did see what Sandra was trying to tell them. Everyone knew exactly who wrote it, as she knew they would. Not all were freed from their burden of hatred. Larry's widow still haunted her physically and mentally. Sandra felt sorry for her knowing how difficult her life must be carrying that weight of contempt.

The landlord sued Sandra for negligence. The claim was that Sandra had allowed access of the property to the perpetrator. She hadn't. She was at work. He did have the same kind of access as any of the neighbors dogs had. He simply had to walk onto the yard. Breaking a window to gain entry put things in an entirely different perspective. It was a clear-cut case of break and enter, arson and suicide. The lawyer for the claimant ended up refusing to carry the case into court after seeing the police report. There was no legal case of negligence.

There was no thought for what Sandra and her children had lost. The landlord was claiming pain and suffering because of the incident. Pain and suffering!! Who's pain and whose suffering? Several people could have lost their lives in that dwelling had the good Lord himself not foreseen what was about to transpire. A friend of Sandra's was in the house as well that night along with a friend of the deceased whom he had left there when he left in a rage. Fortunately, both friends were not there in the morning. Sandra's family had lost everything they owned except the clothes on their backs. Who had pain and suffering?

Negligent? Yes, Sandra was, although none of her negligence could be cured in a courtroom. Flaws in human nature are not necessarily illegal. Everyone has them. Sandra felt she was responsible for putting herself and her family in that kind of position where a mad man could take away their lives with one match. The bottom line was Sandra felt responsible for not listening to her instincts, again.

Sandra and her kids became convinced they could handle anything that life could throw at them from there on.

However they wondered, what more could there possibly be in store for them? Were there any more trials and tribulations left in life that they hadn't already seen?

The answers to those questions didn't become apparent until a few years later.

Sandra and the children began the daunting task of rebuilding their lives. The children were fifteen and sixteen years old.

Bonnie wasn't one of the hand-full Sandra wrote about. She opened her heart and home to the homeless family. In the face of tragedy the two women became friends again.

Susan was in grade twelve. She quit school to go to work to help put a home back together. Steve was working as well. Sandra's employer offered the family a house to rent. The Red Cross gave them blankets and a few other necessities of life. One family donated a bedroom suite. Another loaned a kitchen suite. Other people donated clothing. A collection of money was taken up where Sandra worked. A friend of Sandra's wanted to have a social event to collect money for them, but Sandra declined saying she didn't feel like partying. A co-worker of Sandra's asked her what she needed the most of everyday household things. Sandra told her she needed coat hangers. The woman couldn't believe that was all Sandra wanted. Sandra told her she needed lots of little things that are always taken for granted, but coat hangers would be the most appreciated. She was given a bundle of coat hangers the next day. Beds for the kids were rustled up from somewhere. The kids and Sandra went shopping for a new living room suite. She wanted the family to be able to have something brand new that they could call their own.

Sandra took a week off work after the house fire. When she went back to work the contents on her desk had been left untouched. A pamphlet she had been reading around one o'clock on the day of the fire was still open on her desk. It was a pamphlet about fire safety in the home. It mentioned that every family should have a plan of action, as in a designated meeting area outside the home. Sandra planned to discuss it with Steve and Susan that evening. Together they would design a plan.

This is the premonition the card reader told me about! Sandra realized in amazement as she stared at the open pages of the pamphlet that no one had moved in a week

Chapter Fourteen

Drägo was released from prison about three years later. Sandra's arthritis had gone through her body like a cancer after the house fire. She became disabled and had to retire from her government job.

She was in the hospital getting her second hip replacement the first time she saw Drägo. He had come to the hospital to visit her. They had some contact over the past few years. Sandra had visited him a few times and spoke with him on the telephone. Their last conversation had been about Drägo's dog. The dog became very sick. His back end fell down when he walked. Sandra took him to a vet who told her that the dog wasn't going to survive. He had severe internal injuries that went by undetected from when Drägo had run over him. Sandra had the dog put down. Drägo was livid because he wouldn't believe there was anything wrong with the dog. He had a picture of Sandra in his jail cell. He tore it in half and sent it to her in the mail without saying a word.

When Susan seen it, she was horrified and said, "That means murder, Mom!"

Susan and Steve seldom visited Drägo during that stint in prison. They were tired of seeing him in prison. They felt that visiting him was a way of condoning the reason he was there. Sandra agreed with her children's assessment, but had still made the occasional visit.

After a week in the hospital, Sandra went home with discharge orders to attend physiotherapy sessions. A few months later she had both knees replaced at the same time. Sandra felt like someone had broken both of her legs. She was in excruciating pain most of the time for weeks after the surgeries. More physiotherapy was in order. Sandra had moved into an apartment in Riverside because she wasn't able to drive herself to the sessions. She traveled to and from appointments via a handy van service for the disabled.

Sandra had recovered from the excruciating pain by the time the authorities came into the picture again, but still couldn't walk without some kind of an aid. She recalled wheeling herself in her wheelchair to get to the phone whenever Bill called her. One time she didn't make it to the phone before it quit ringing. It only rang three times. Within a few minutes it rang again. It was Bill. Sandra asked if he had called a few minutes earlier. He said he had. Sandra had to remind him that it took some time for her to get to the phone. She couldn't always make it in three rings. Bill apologized saying he forgot and that he was in a frenzy, so he wasn't thinking straight.

Drägo was on a crime spree in a distant part of the area. The police were right on his tail, but still couldn't catch him red handed. Of course there was still no evidence at any of the crime scenes to indicate exactly who the criminal was except Drägo's MO. That left no choice but to catch Drägo in the act.

During that spree, Bill had the second site Sandra had shown the police excavated. He had been on Drägo's trail all night. He called Sandra in the morning when the team returned to Riverside telling her about the antics of the night before. She knew full well they would have pulled out the night vision equipment. Meanwhile another police department had taken over the surveillance temporarily. During the night, Drägo had parked his car and gone to sleep. The police watched. A woman walked up to Drägo's car. Always on guard Drägo woke up right away. The woman asked him for a light for her cigarette. Drägo gave her one. She was looking for a little action as well and didn't want to leave him alone. It took some doing, but Drägo was able to politely shoo her away and went back to sleep. He usually had a way with the ladies.

Sandra thought of one incident when she had to rescue Drägo from a woman. He seldom drank alcohol because he had to keep his wits about him at all times, but Sandra and Drägo were in a classy bar in downtown Riverside. While Drägo was standing at the bar getting drinks for them, a classy looking lady of the night exuding confidence approached him. He didn't know what to do or say. Sandra wasn't far away sitting at a table. She had seen the woman zero in on Drägo as soon as they came in the door. She watched the woman head directly for him at the bar. He hadn't noticed any of the previous action. He stood at the bar looking back and forth from Sandra to the woman looking absolutely perplexed. The woman had propositioned him. Sandra took pity and was pissed off with the woman. Being temporarily crippled didn't turn her into chopped liver.

She got on her canes, wobbled up to the woman, stood face to face with her wearing an icy glare and spit, "Back off!"

The woman's demeanor instantly changed, her confidence shattered. She literally backed away and eyed Sandra as if she was a lunatic. Sandra watched the woman retreat from her icy glare. Drägo looked at Sandra amazed.

As the woman left the bar he said, "Good job! I really didn't know what to do with her."

As they both started laughing, Sandra said, "I could see that."

When they got back to Sandra's apartment, Drägo said to Steve, "Guess what your mother did tonight."

"Oh! That's a tough one! Give me something easier," Steve said, smiling.

When Drägo told him how Sandra had chased off a prostitute, Steve beamed, "Yep! That's my mom!"

While Sandra was still on the phone with Bill after he had returned from parts unknown, she asked him what he was doing at work, why he wasn't sleeping after being out all night. He told her his night wasn't over yet. It was nine o'clock in the morning.

When Sandra questioned him about that he said, "I'm going to make a withdrawal."

The equipment operator hired for the excavation of the wooded area thought he was looking for a dead body. The police let him think what he liked because they didn't want to reveal what they were looking for. Bill called that afternoon and asked Sandra to go to the site. Steve drove her there. The trees on the five acre wooded site had all been uprooted. There were huge mounds of dirt and caverns it had come out of everywhere. The place looked like it had been bombed. Sandra wondered why it was excavated before Drägo was captured? He might see it. It was too late for damage control. The damage had already been done, for better or for worse.

Drägo hadn't been around for a while at that point. He wasn't in Riverside either. Bill called Sandra one day to say that an off duty policeman had spotted Drägo in a small town about two hours east of Riverside. The officer recognized Drägo on sight and immediately lit into chasing him. Drägo jumped on a train that just happened to be moving very slowly through the small community. Bill told Sandra about the chase and that Drägo was on the run. Several police officers were involved in the manhunt.

"Which direction is that train headed?" Sandra asked nervously.

"West," Bill dreaded telling her.

"West! When is it due in Riverside?!" Sandra panicked.

"It's due in two hours," Bill said reluctantly.

"Oh my gawd, Bill, that train can't get here! Drägo will see the excavation that was done! I will be killed!" she shouted into the phone panic stricken.

"I know what you're saying, Sandra," Bill replied with panic riddling his voice as well.

"Tell them they have to search the train! The tanker cars! The damn tanker cars!" Sandra stuttered, while screaming into the phone.

Bill's voice rose as well, "Sandra what do you mean by the tanker cars? What are you talking about?"

"Oh damn I can't think of the right name for them," she said.

"The, the," she was wracking her brain hoping the words would come to her with starting the sentence.

"What Sandra?" Bill asked, trying to hide his impatience but not succeeding.

"The grain cars!" she yelled as if a light has just snapped on.

She heard Bill's impatience with her. Hell, she was impatient with herself because she couldn't find the words she needed in her panic stricken state. Bill knew she had something very important to tell him about the train. He had to get the woman who was stuttering and screaming to get a grip on herself.

What about the grain cars?" Bill asked in an agitated expectant voice.

"The hole in the back of them! That's where Drägo travels when he jumps on a train! He always jokes and says the holes look small from the outside, but inside they could sleep six!" she shouted into the phone. She was thankful the words were coming to her.

Bill thanked her rushing to get off the phone saying he had to call the attending department. The police ordered the train stopped. It was searched from one end to the other. Drägo wasn't found. Bill called Sandra again about two hours later.

"Drägo got away again," he told her in a timid disappointed voice.

Sandra couldn't contain the incredulous tone in her voice.

"What do you mean, he got away again? This just can't keep happening! Did they search the damn train?" she found herself yelling again.

"Yes they did. They stopped it and searched it thoroughly," he told her still quiet and upset, but letting Sandra sound off.

"Are you sure it was a thorough search, Bill, or are we just taking their word for it because they lost him? Did they check every hole? Every nook and cranny?" she asked in exasperation and disbelief.

"The swat team from Craney moved in. There were police officers swarming over every inch of the train. They checked absolutely everywhere that a man could possibly fit. They used a long heavy metal rod ramming it mercilessly into every hole several times. Believe me if Drägo had been in one of them, he couldn't have helped but yell out in pain," Bill said. "He must have jumped off the train at the other end of town before it was stopped."

"Oh for crissake! Sandra yelled. "This just can't be happening! He cannot get to Riverside! I repeat! I am dead meat if he does! You of all people know what I am saying."

Bill attempted to console her. "There are three police departments and a team of dogs searching the area right now. He has to be in that town somewhere. I know Drägo's good, but he couldn't have just evaporated. Don't worry, Sandra, they will get him."

Sandra wasn't consoled. It wouldn't be the first time Drägo had outsmarted a police sting. Maybe the dogs would be able to do something, she hoped. She also thought about the jackass cop who lit chase after him.

Why would one cop do that? She wondered. *Isn't that just plain stupid*?

Given the fact that the officer recognized Drägo on sight he obviously knew about Drägo and his eccentric habits. Drägo was there to case the small town and would never do anything in the daylight hours. Drägo always cased towns. Sandra had seen him doing it. Susan was really pissed off one time when she noticed Drägo doing that when the family was out for dinner one evening in a small town outside of Riverside. Watch him. See where he goes. What was the cop thinking? Why not call for back up after he knew Drägo was either in a hotel room or restaurant, his favorite haunts?

But no! Sandra thought. "*The jack ass put everybody in a helluva position by trying to be a hero. My gawd*! *Will this never end*?

"I bloody well hope they get him this time. If they don't, you're going to have to send someone to keep me under police protection until they do," she warned Bill.

"I know what you're saying, Sandra. I have to get back to them right now to see what's going on. I'll keep you posted," he told her.

Sandra was absolutely frantic. She wanted to run and hide but was in no condition to be running anywhere. She was powerless to do anything but wait for Bill to call her back and hope to hell he called her before Drägo seen the excavation. She was at home alone.

Four grueling hours later the phone rang. Sandra grabbed it immediately. She had sat right beside it since Bill's last call.

"They got him!" Bill shouted, skipping the formality of saying hello.

"Oh, thank God!" Sandra sighed in relief.

"Yep, the dogs cornered him in a garden shed in somebody's back yard," he told Sandra.

She could hear the relief in his voice.

"Is he ok?" Sandra asked. She hated to think of Drägo being chewed on by a police dog.

"He's exhausted, but other than that he's fine. He didn't even put up a fight." Bill said, "The nightmare is over, Sandra."

"Not soon enough for me, Bill. This has been absolute hell for me right from the start. It's the hardest thing I have ever had to do in my life," Sandra told him.

"I know, Sandra, but you can relax now." Bill's tone of voice emitted sympathy.

"Ok, I'll try," she told him. "I just hope that jail can hold him. We can't have him escaping and have to go through anything like this all over again."

"I agree, Sandra," Bill said.

The conversation ended. Bill prepared for yet another road trip. Sandra sat in her wheelchair and sobbed uncontrollably.

Chapter Fifteen

Drägo was held in a minimum-security jail in Craney not far from where he was arrested. The security status of the prison concerned Sandra. She thought about the time Drägo had escaped from a maximum-security penitentiary. Drägo was to remain in jail until he went to court on eighty-three charges of breaking and enter and theft.

Bill got to the prison two hours after he talked to Sandra. He talked to Drägo right away.

He said to Drägo, "For every minute you were in your car over the past months, so was I."

"Well then, man, you deserve this one!" Drägo said.

Did Bill forget to mention the rest of the surveillance team?

Within the week a newspaper headline read, "The Police Got The Man and the Loot."

Bill visited Sandra a few days later and told her what Drägo had said to him.

"You know, Sandra, I believe he was sincere when he said that to me," Bill said.

"Oh for sure, he would have been," Sandra told him. "He knows the hell he puts the police through. He figures that anyone that can catch him is a hero."

Within hours of the arrest, Sandra had called the police officer with the sense of humor who came to her apartment with Randy originally. Dick worked in the jurisdiction where Drägo had been arrested. He was the arresting officer. Again, he had caught Drägo. Bill told Sandra that he was the arresting officer. She wondered how that could be when she knew that he was in his office burning up the telephone lines between her and the capturing division. It really didn't matter to Sandra. Drägo was caught and that's all that was important.

Sandra was concerned about Drägo's well being. She hoped Dick would tell her. He was happy to hear from Sandra. He had wanted to contact her before that, but Bill told him to leave her alone because of a run-in with Riverside city police. Sandra didn't want every cop who had an interest in Drägo showing up at her door.

"Cripes," she said to Bill, "half of the eastern police departments would be here in that case."

She also told Bill that she wouldn't speak to anyone but him about Drägo. The cop thanked her, very proudly.

Sandra made a comment to Dick about Drägo's well being and then said, "But I guess there's no one there that likes him much, so there's no point voicing my concern to anyone there."

"No, no. Quite the contrary, Sandra, we have a great respect for the guy. Some of us have even come to like him. He never carried a weapon and was never violent toward any of us or anyone he stole from. We learned a lot from him during the course of the investigation. He's a brilliant man. It's just too bad that he has never used his brains toward something legal. He could have been a millionaire by now. He is cooperating fully with us. Everything is calm. There's nothing to worry about," the officer assured Sandra.

Then in a hushed tone he said, "Oh damn, I have to go. Bill is coming. He doesn't want me talking to you."

That wasn't the first time a police officer had commented to Sandra about Drägo's brilliance. The general consensus was always the same. Drägo could have been a millionaire legally a few times over. During the investigation, at his supervisor's request, Bill had asked Sandra to speak to Drägo on behalf of the police department.

"The cops were here today," Sandra told Drägo, during one of his regular visits.

"Oh, what did they want?" Drägo asked, not looking impressed or surprised.

"They want you to work for them, instead of against them," she answered.

"Ya, right! Doing what?" Drägo asked her with a skeptical tone.

"They want you to train business owners about security in their establishments and maybe even talk to kids in schools about the hazards of criminal life," she said.

Sandra hoped Drägo would take the police up on their offer, but she had her doubts.

"What the hell do they think I am, a damn snitch? That would be like turning in my friends," Drägo told her. "If you see them again tell them the answer is no."

Sandra wasn't at all surprised by his response. A different response would have surprised her, but she thought it was worth a shot. Drägo had surprised her before. Bill and Sandra had discussed the "honor amongst thieves" issue before that. Bill said most people had no idea of just how true that old adage is and the enormity of it. Sandra agreed. She had seen it too many times. She knew there was nothing a thief wouldn't do for another one. Sandra had also noticed that a thief could pick another one out of a crowd. They had some kind of invisible bond or vibe between them that law-abiding people couldn't detect. Nothing could sever it unless one became a snitch. God help him or her!

Chapter Sixteen

When Drägo was on the lam, he called Sandra and asked her to get his things out of a hotel room that he rented on a monthly basis. The rent was due and the heat was intense, so he wouldn't be able to get back to pay the rent he told her. He didn't say where he was. Sandra knew there was no point in asking him. It was a rare call. He seldom called when he was on the lam and was very brief when he did after the cross border episode. Bill used to ask Sandra frequently during those times if she had heard from Drägo.

She always answered, "Not a peep." That saying almost became a joke between them.

There was no such thing as caller ID or anything like it at the time. A telephone wasn't one of Drägo's favorite tools to start with. He would have seldom used one if modern day technology had been available at the time. The caller ID feature became available within a year. Sandra got the feature as soon as it was available.

She remembers saying to Steve, "Your dad would just hate this."

Steve chuckled in agreement.

Sandra called Bill and told him about Drägo's request to remove his things from the hotel room. She asked him if he anticipated any problems with her doing that. The reason for the call was actually two fold. Sandra wanted the law to be aware of what she was doing and why. She didn't want anyone thinking she was doing anything shady. He told her to go ahead because he didn't see a problem. He would tell the rest of the police team what she was going to do to avoid any problems.

Sandra and Steve went to the hotel. Sandra thought Steve should be there because he had ID to prove that he was Drägo's son. One look at him showed that as well. Sandra had nothing to prove she was even remotely associated with Drägo. The hotel owner let them remove Drägo's belongings after Steve showed his ID. The owner was polite when he told them he would have to call the city police informing them. They had instructed him to call them if anyone showed up for Drägo's things.

"That's understandable," Sandra said to the owner.

"Yes, we have no problem with that," Steve said, verifying that he was in agreement.

Within about an hour of Steve and Sandra getting home with Drägo's things there was a bold knock on the apartment door. Sandra and Steve looked at each other, but never said a word. They both recognized the knocking of a cop. Steve answered the door.

He was cordial and didn't hesitate to invite the two plain clothed city police officers inside after they introduced themselves.

As a form of introduction and an attempt to keep things light Steve said, "I'm the product of the fellow you're looking for."

Neither cop acknowledged that he had said anything.

"Somebody from here picked up Drägo Stepano's belongings today," one officer said right away.

"Yes, my mother and I did," Steve said to him as he indicated toward Sandra who was sitting quietly at the kitchen table.

"So, where is Stepano?" the cop asked.

"We don't know," Steve told him without hesitation.

There was a little more chit chatting between the officer and Steve before the other cop spoke up. The good cop, bad cop routine happened.

"Ya, right! You people don't know where he is! We don't believe that! Just tell us where he is before we charge both of you with obstruction of justice!" the cop said, trying to sound intimidating.

Sandra hated that tone. It was her cue. She had deliberately said nothing wanting the cops to think she was a mousy little woman. She had been curious as to what direction the conversation was going to take. If she hadn't heard that tone she may well have sat there and said nothing, but when she heard it she became livid.

She jumped out of her chair and shouted, "My son has told you that we don't know where his father is! We don't question him about his whereabouts over the telephone because he wouldn't tell us anyway! Don't you dare stand there trying to threaten us with your bullshit intimidation and calling us liars! If anyone is doing anything wrong here, it's you people because you are interfering in a national investigation!"

She remained standing. The cops were stunned by the sudden outburst from the quiet looking little woman. The bad cop had to think fast.

He regained himself and yelled back at her, "As long as he's in our city we have an interest in him!"

"Well, he's not in your city but that's all we know! We don't know where he is! I took the police to a stash of stolen money! Now you have the gall to stand in my home accusing my son and I of lying to the police! You get to hell out of here before I call the real cops!" Sandra shouted back, glaring from one to the other of the tall officers.

Her eyes challenged them to speak again. Both police officers turned at the same time and left the apartment. Sandra was outraged. She immediately got on the phone and started shouting in Bill's ear. He had never heard her really angry before.

As soon as Sandra heard his voice on the phone she yelled, "Bill, I am so mad I could just spit nickels!"

"What's wrong, Sandra?" he asked her with true concern and dismay.

"Steve and I picked up Drägo's stuff today. Two city cops were just here accusing us of lying to them about Drägo's whereabouts. They said they could charge us with obstruction of justice!" she told him.

"Did you tell them anything, Sandra?" he asked.

"I told them I had taken you to a stash of stolen money, so Steve and I could hardly be accused of collaborating with a criminal!" she said, still shouting.

"Oh, Sandra, I wish you hadn't told them that," Bill's voice sank.

"Well, it's too late now! I didn't have a helluva lot of choice! They were not going to get away with calling Steve and I liars after all we have been through trying to help the authorities," Sandra told him.

"You can't tell anyone about this, Sandra! You can't even trust another cop!" Bill told her, stressing the importance of absolute silence.

"Did you tell them anything else?" Bill asked her as if he was afraid to hear the answer.

"Yes, I did. I told them to get to hell out because they are interfering in a national investigation!" she said.

Sandra thought she detected a muffled chuckle. Bill asked her if she knew which division they were from. She said she didn't know or care. Bill said he would find out.

"You do that and when you do you tell them to stay right to hell away from us!" Sandra was close to shrieking again.

"It's ok, Sandra, calm down," Bill said in a calming voice but she thought she could hear amusement as well. "I will tell them not to bother you again."

"Thank you! I gotta go now, so I can stop screaming in your ear. I'm sorry about that, but I'm just vicious here!" she told Bill.

"That's ok, Sandra. It comes with the badge. I'm glad you called," Bill said with a definite chuckle.

Sandra never saw the city police at her door again.

After Drägo's arrest, he called Sandra from the jail. He asked her to bring some of his clothes and his TV to the prison. Sandra said she would. She called Bill to tell him what she was going to do. She felt stupid calling to tell him because she was sure he knew all about any telephone conversations she had. A few calls she had made to Bill were strictly a formality.

Sandra drove three hours go get to the prison that housed Drägo. Her car was packed with the things he had requested. After signing in, she waited in the visiting room for a guard to escort Drägo in.

Drägo was glad to see her. She was glad to see him. Even so, she knew she had to think about every word she said to Drägo before she opened her mouth. She was afraid of giving herself away. Drägo told her that the police had found his money. He reminded her of the city police being on the road on Groundhog Day and said someone must have reported him digging.

"I was only four inches from it when I was digging!" he exclaimed.

"Four inches!" Sandra said before she cut the sentence short.

She almost added, "It was more like forty feet!"

"Yep! Isn't that a bugger?" Drägo asked her.

"Ya, that's a bugger all right," Sandra said as if she totally agreed with him.

There was some more chatter about Drägo's pending court date and the like. Then their conversation took on a whole different twist. Drägo started mumbling in his stealth mode tone to Sandra.

"I've decided I don't like the accommodations around here, so I'm going to be checking myself out," he told her.

"Oh! How do you plan on doing that?" she asked him, attempting to sound casual. Sandra was alarmed but didn't dare show it.

"The security here is a joke," Drägo whispered.

"They are going to be transferring me to the pen soon to wait for my court date. They don't want to keep me here because they think I'm an escape risk," Drägo told her as he looked around to see if anyone was within earshot.

"I will get an exercise period in the yard before they come for me. I will be leaving from there," he said, still looking around warily. "I've checked it all out. It will be a snap."

Sandra had little to say. She only said enough to let Drägo know that she acknowledged what he was telling her. She didn't agree nor disagree. Drägo thought her silence was for security reasons. She was mortified and hardly dared to open her mouth for fear of what might come out.

The visit ended. Drägo thanked her for bringing his things and telling her that it looked good on his resume. No one would suspect he didn't plan on staying. Having her bring his stuff would make it look as if he was settling in. Sandra thought about the fact that Drägo had an ulterior motive in everything he did; often using her like a pawn. A hug later, they separated. Drägo went back into the bowels of the prison. Sandra went straight to the nearest police station. Her worst nightmare was about to become a reality if she didn't do something about it.

Luck seemed to be on Sandra's side for a change because she was in Dick's jurisdiction. She had to find him even if he wasn't on duty because she wouldn't tell anyone else what she knew. Arriving at the police station she almost ran into the building. She asked the receptionist if the officer was there. Sandra couldn't remember his last name. She told the receptionist it was a long name that seemed to have every letter of the alphabet in it. The receptionist smiled and directed Sandra to an office across the hall.

"He's in there," she told Sandra.

Sandra went to the office door and looked inside. Dick was sitting at a desk. He looked up when he noticed movement in the doorway.

"Well, hello, Sandra! What brings you here?" he was surprised to see her.

"I just came from visiting Drägo at the prison. He said he doesn't like his accommodations so he's going to check himself out," she told him.

"Oh, really! Did he say how he plans on pulling that off?" he asked Sandra intrigued.

Sandra told him exactly what Drägo had said to her. The officer was concerned as well. After all, he had been the one to chase Drägo down when he had escaped from the penitentiary years earlier. Sandra knew she was talking to the right police officer. He would take her seriously where others might not. She didn't care what Bill would think about the fact that she didn't go to him with the information first.

The cop got on the phone right away. He called the warden of the prison where Drägo was.

"I have been told that Drägo Stepano is planning an escape from your establishment," he warned the Warden.

Of course Sandra could only hear Dick's side of the conversation.

"Oh no, this is no rumor," Dick said. "I was made aware of this by an excellent source who just came from visiting Stepano at the prison. He told my source about his plan."

The officer got off the phone. He looked at Sandra who was looking worried and forlorn.

He tried to console her by saying, "Don't worry, Sandra, he won't get away on us again. The prison has been informed of the situation so they will know what to do to avoid it. I really want to thank you for coming to tell me though. You did the right thing."

Sandra thanked him for taking her seriously and taking immediate action. She left to get on the highway for the long drive home. She had lots of time to think. That wasn't always a good thing. Sandra shouldn't have been driving. She was very stressed. Sorrow dripped down her cheeks.

Sandra called Bill when she got home and told him what had transpired during the day. He asked her why she had gone into the local police department instead of just calling him when she got home. Bill sounded dejected. She told him she felt she had to talk to the officer who had been involved in a prior escape of Drägo's and someone from that jurisdiction. She said she wanted to make sure that no one brushed the information off. Bill claimed he would never have brushed it off. Maybe not but Sandra wasn't about to take any chances. She thought she might have sounded paranoid to anyone else but Dick, not to mention she wanted to unload the burden Drägo had put on her shoulders to someone else immediately. Bill wasn't happy. Sandra didn't care. It was her life that that would be snuffed out if Drägo ever got the chance to see the excavated area.

The normal routine when transferring prisoners from that particular prison was to let the inmate know what day he would be transferred. The inmate was always allowed to have an exercise period just before the trip. Drägo had told Sandra about that so that's exactly what he was counting on. He would be vacating the premises from the exercise yard. Prison officials told Drägo the date his transfer would take place.

Drägo phoned Sandra from the penitentiary a week or so after he had told her about his scheme. He called to tell her where he was and that his plan to escape had been foiled. Sandra asked what happened. She had to sound like she was sympathizing with Drägo.

"It didn't work because they didn't transfer me the day they said they would. Some guards walked up to me out of the blue two days before and told me that plans had changed. I was being transferred right then and there. When I told them I wanted to exercise in the yard first, they said there wasn't time because the van was running with two other prisoners waiting inside. I had to go with them right on the spot.

I couldn't believe it. I was really pissed off, but what could I do?" Drägo said.

Sandra sympathized. She couldn't believe he didn't ask her if she had said anything to anyone. He didn't even suspect anything like it. Drägo really thought it was just a case of a change in plans as he had been told. It was an odd change of plans though because prisons are known for their rigid routine. It is seldom broken.

At the end of the conversation Drägo asked Sandra to visit him in the penitentiary. She said she would. Before she went she called Bill because she knew the authorities could see her name on the visiting list if they looked and they would look. She had every reason to think they might be watching to see who was visiting Drägo. Bill's attitude on the phone confirmed that suspicion.

"Why are you going to visit him?" Bill asked her, sounding like he couldn't believe it.

"Because he asked me to," Sandra told him. "How was I supposed to say no? I thought we are still trying to keep him from suspecting anything of me," Sandra said, not liking the avenue the conversation had taken nor Bill's tone.

Sandra went to visit Drägo a few times before he whispered to her again in an outside courtyard just off the visiting room. Her heart almost stopped when he started telling her about another plan of escape.

My gawd when is this going to stop? she thought.

She was very distraught, but again she couldn't let Drägo see any indication of it. She feared she might lose it right then and there. She knew her life depended on vigilant self-control. Sandra didn't know how much longer she could keep that up. She listened carefully as Drägo told her the plot. He sounded proud of himself when he told her that a magnet screwed up cameras. Sandra looked at him confused. She needed to know exactly what he was talking about.

"If you stick a magnet on any camera it screws it right up. The picture on the monitors turns completely to snow," he explained to her, "I've only got one problem with my plan that I haven't figured out yet."

"What's that?" she asked, making every effort to sound casual, but not overly interested at the same time.

"There's a camera in the exercise yard that is fifty feet in the air. I haven't figured out how I'm going to get to it yet. The rest of them are simple, but that one poses a problem," he continued, explaining his plot to Sandra.

"But never fear," he chuckled, "I will figure it out."

"I don't doubt you will," Sandra said with an emphasis that could be taken in any way or as if she was cheering him on.

Sandra had every reason to believe Drägo. He was in the same prison he had escaped from years earlier. Security had been beefed up since then, but Sandra still worried. The man was absolutely relentless in his quest for freedom and crime. Sandra knew her life would go to hell in a hand basket if he managed to escape. At the least, her and her kids would be under constant surveillance again. Barely able to contain herself she ended the visit after what she hoped was an inconspicuous amount of time. Drägo thought nothing of it. She needed to be alone so she could think. Sandra was absolutely devastated by the secret Drägo burdened her with again. She felt like she wanted to crawl into a dark hole and stay there until life passed her by. She drove home wiping tears from her eyes again.

Sandra thought long and hard before she called Bill because it seemed to her that he was being careless since Drägo was incarcerated. She finally did tell him about Drägo's plan. She didn't know what else to do except continue fighting for her life. Bill was concerned about what Sandra told him. He assured her that he would fix it without implicating her. She had expressed fear of being implicated. She was sure she was the only person that Drägo had told. It just happened that Bill was going on a police department tour of the penitentiary the following day. He said he would have a discreet word with the warden while he was there.

Bill called Sandra the next day after the tour. He was excited.

"I seen the camera Drägo was talking about in the exercise yard. I even saw him in one of the work shops. He looked right at me. He's right. The camera is fifty feet in the air. I don't see how he could ever get near it, but I mentioned it to the warden anyway when I told him about the escape plan," he told her, sounding pleased with himself.

Sandra freaked out. "You told him specifically about the cameras? Are you crazy?"

"I had to Sandra. How else could I have told him about Drägo's scheme?" he asked quite shocked by her response.

Sandra sat holding the phone shaking her head in disbelief.

"What if one of the guards say something to Drägo about the cameras?" she asked. "Who the hell would know anything about any of the cameras other than me?"

"The guards won't say anything. The warden assured me that he would keep the information to himself," Bill told her.

She wondered how the warden could make such a claim and prevent Drägo from escaping at the same time. Was he going to make it his own personal assignment to follow Drägo around the prison watching for him to go near a camera? Sandra didn't want to talk about it anymore. She was too upset. She ended the conversation with Bill abruptly. Neither one of them were happy.

Sandra didn't hear from Drägo for almost a month. She stewed in the juices of fear and the grip of anxiety for the entire time.

When Drägo did finally call her he asked if she had said anything about the cameras to anyone.

"Why the hell would I do that?" she asked, carefully trying not to protest too much.

"Ya, I know. I'm sorry for even asking, but I had to ask. You know how it is. I know where it came from then," Drägo said.

"I was in the yard one day after that and two guards walked up and grabbed me. They put me in shackles and threw me into the hole." Drägo told her, "That's why I haven't called you for a while. I've been in the hole ever since. When they let me out they told me to make sure I didn't go near any cameras."

Sandra was sure she would vomit into the pit of despair. She had paced for weeks wondering why she hadn't heard from Drägo. She asked Bill if he had heard anything.

"Not a peep," he said.

Drägo's spirits sounded good, but she imagined him in solitary confinement for a month wondering why he was there. That gave him way too much time to think. She hated the idea that she was responsible and had to lie to save her life. She thought about Bill. Had he lied to her about the warden's reaction to Drägo's story? Did the warden lie to Bill? Damn it! Who could she trust? Didn't both cop and warden know the position they could have put Sandra in? She was angry with both of them and felt like seeing the Warden herself and giving him hell. She was afraid because she didn't know the lay of the land at the prison. One of the inmates might spot her and tell Drägo she was there. Otherwise she would have visited the Warden. She could hardly believe that her life was just as stressful with Drägo in jail as it was with him out. What was she going to do to reclaim her life? The only thing that came to mind was she had to sever herself from Drägo completely again, which was her long-term plan. She knew she had to do it gradually though so as not to arouse suspicion. Again, visits became fewer and further between until they stopped completely.

Drägo still called Sandra occasionally, but didn't ask her to visit. He assumed she was like the kids and just fed up with going in and out of a prison visiting room to see him. She had to keep her wits about her whenever Drägo called. Since he didn't have much of a future in jail, he kept talking about past events. Sandra had to think about every word she said to him making sure she never slipped up regarding those events. It was very nerve wracking for her. She prayed Drägo would never notice her tension and that she would be able to keep a reign on her lethal tongue. Sandra wondered if the card reader had seen just how "lethal" lethal could be.

Chapter Seventeen

A year went by, Sandra was surprised when she answered the phone one day and heard Bill's voice. Her furry at him had subsided. After all, she had survived and lied her way around the unfortunate incident. Bill called to tell her that he had received a promotion at work. His new position gave him the equivalency of the FBI. Sandra thought that comparison was odd because when she first started working with Bill he told her that he was the equivalent to the FBI. Sandra let it go so as not to burst his bubble. Bill was very happy. Sandra was truly happy for him. She told Bill that if Drägo escaped from jail again or was released she would be looking for him no matter what department he was in. Bill was the only one who could help her she had decided. He was the best she had to work with, so she would have to make do. She didn't want to have to start all over training another cop if she needed help again.

"I don't care if you're stationed on the other side of the country. Riverside department will have to haul your butt back here because I won't work with anyone else when it comes to Drägo," Sandra said, "apologize to your wife and kids in advance for me."

Bill sounded proud when he said, "Thank you, Sandra, but I hope for everyone's sake that he doesn't escape. I hope we all get a few years reprieve now. Oh, before I forget there's something else I've wanted to tell you. We found out why Drägo only works in small towns. He rattles the door of a business just enough to set the alarm off and then he runs away and hides watching the local department arrive. They usually sleep at night in small police departments and only go out when they are called. Drägo knows that. He rattles the same door after the members are back at their station, tripping the alarm again. So, they show up again. The third time the alarm goes off they don't bother to go out because it must be another false alarm. When Drägo trips the alarm for the third time he is actually entering the building. He's really sharp ya know. We've watched him driving other departments crazy. They don't even know we are there watching."

Sandra was happy to hear that quirk of Drägo's had been figured out. It had been a mystery to her for years. She wanted to ask Drägo about it, but she thought that might be getting too close to the heart of the situation arousing suspicion. She also thought she would leave it up to the police to figure it out. She had told them about it. That was good enough. Sandra left it up to them to discover the reasoning behind it. Both Sandra and the police knew it was an important point, but it took a long time to figure out why it was so important. Sandra found out years later that Steve knew the reasoning behind Drägo's quirk, but he thought it was so obvious that he never guessed it was such a mystery.

Sandra had news of her own to tell Bill but it paled in comparison. She still thought it was worth telling him. She told him that she had changed her last name. Bill wanted to know what it was changed to and why she had done that. She told him what her new name was. She told him the reason for the change was because she had lost her ID. Sandra decided to replace it with her mother's maiden name in memory of the women on her mother's side. She felt Bill should know about the change in case of any problems in the future. The conversation ended with Bill basically telling her to have a good life.

Bill knew that Sandra had gone through absolute hell to get Drägo out of her family's life. The capture happened within a few months of Sandra starting to work with the police for the common goal between them. Bill told Sandra that she had saved the department hundreds of thousands of dollars in manpower alone by helping them. He was aware that the capture of Drägo usually took a few years. Was Bill telling Sandra they couldn't have done it without her in such a short time? Or at all? Of course he couldn't say that. He did tell her that if there was anything he could ever do for her she was to let him know.

A year or so later Steve and Sandra were watching the evening news when a particular story caught their attention. The news broadcaster said there had been a large sum of money found by a railroad track near a small town in an eastern part of the country. Nothing more was said about it. Sandra and Steve looked at each other immediately after the short broadcast ended. They smiled at each other. Steve was the first to speak.

"Well! We know who put that there," he said.

"Yep, we sure do," Sandra agreed.

She was tempted to call Bill to see if he knew anything about it but didn't bother. Sandra imagined the local police department painstakingly finger printing every bill as had been done with the seventy five thousand in Riverside. The legend of Drägo would be around for a long time. Fortunately, there is no "best before" date on money. The police, Steve and Sandra suspected there were several stashes around. In a few months, Drägo had stolen hundreds of thousands of dollars.

Chapter Eighteen

The apartment building the family lived in at the time that Drägo was on the loose was massive. There were four hundred and fifty apartments in it. There were zillions of nooks and crannies within the building with several maintenance rooms and the like. Sandra had seen Drägo checking out a lock on a boiler room door.

Drägo was at the apartment one afternoon when Susan and Sandra were getting ready to leave for the weekend. They were taking a trip across an international border. Sandra had informed Bill about the trip because she anticipated problems crossing the border because they were driving a marked vehicle. Drägo had driven the car too many times. She told him that Drägo wouldn't be in the trunk of the car. She was half-assed joking when she said it, but she knew if she didn't tell the police about the trip her and Susan could run into serious problems. The mother and daughter were taking a well-deserved trip getting away from all the chaos. They hated the fact that they had to report to the police before hand.

Drägo left the apartment a few minutes before they did. When they went outside to go to the car, Sandra noticed that Drägo's car was still on the parking lot of the building. He was nowhere to be seen. Sandra thought that was a curious situation. It concerned her. What was he up to? She didn't know, but she felt she should call Bill and mention it to him. Sandra called Bill from a drug store several blocks away from the apartment building.

She hadn't seen a phone booth a safe distance away from the building. She pulled Randy's trick and flashed a policeman's business card in a pharmacist's face saying, "I have to call these people."

A few police business cards were the only evidence that she was working against Drägo. Sandra carried that evidence with her. Bill told her that Drägo was still in her apartment building.

"There's something up with that Bill because he left our apartment before we did wanting us to think he was gone but I see that his car is still there. I don't know what the hell he's up to but just to let you know, I left him a key for the apartment," she told him.

"He could be up to just about anything, Sandra. It's a helluva big building. I hope he doesn't have a stash of money in there because we would never find it. It would be like looking for a needle in a haystack, literally," Bill told her.

"That's a true story," Sandra said.

"Ok, we'll keep a close eye on him. You and Susan have a good weekend and I'll talk to you when you get back," said Bill.

"Thanks, we'll give it our best shot," Sandra said.

No one ever found out what Drägo was doing inside the apartment building that day. The incident reminded Sandra of another one when she was still in the wheelchair.

It was one of those usual times when Drägo had taken Sandra out for coffee or someplace. When they got back to her apartment her wheelchair was left on the mat by the door to drip dry. Sandra noticed Drägo eyeing up the many hollow tubular bars of the wheelchair. He looked it over carefully and even looked underneath the seat of it. Then he started feeling around an end cap on one of the bars.

"Don't even think about it!" Sandra told Drägo with a knowing scowl on her face.

He looked at her and smiled because he knew that she knew exactly what he was thinking. Who could have ever forgotten the flashlight incident? Drägo had learned many years earlier that it wasn't a good plan to be carrying a lot of cash on him. He had been convicted before when he was found carrying a stash of money. So to Drägo it was like carrying around evidence. He was constantly on the lookout for hiding places. Everywhere and anywhere became a potential vault in Drägo's criminal rationale. Sandra couldn't believe the wheel chair thing though. Was there no place sacred? Apparently not.

Before Sandra became an informant for the police, she was out with Drägo in his car one afternoon. She was wearing a winter coat that had huge pockets that almost met each other in the middle like a hooded sweatshirt.

Drägo complimented her on the coat saying, "It has really nice pockets."

Sandra thanked him for the unexpected and odd compliment. Then Drägo pulled into a back alley in downtown Riverside, a seedy part of the city. He said he had to go somewhere, but wouldn't be long. Sandra complained and suggested he at least park her on the street instead of the alley. His insistence about leaving the car in the alley made it obvious to her that he didn't want her to see exactly where he was going. She couldn't walk at the time without canes. Her wheelchair was in the trunk. Sandra didn't appreciate sitting in a back alley defenseless.

As if it wasn't enough for Sandra to have to wait in a back alley alone, Drägo made matters worse. He stuffed ten thousand dollars into her pockets before he got out of the car. That was the minute that Sandra knew that something had to be done about Drägo. He had involved her in his criminal career for the first time.

After thinking, *you son-of-a-bitch*, her next thought was of her kids.

Sandra feared he might do something similar with one or both of them at some point. She had the evidence of his crimes in her pockets.

Chapter Nineteen

Immigration was consoled by Drägo's imprisonment, but not pacified. However, it did give them time to get their act together because they had an agenda of their own. It didn't surface until Drägo had been in prison for a year. Immigration wanted to deport him to Europe. It had been a threat for many years that was never carried out. Drägo was well aware of the threat. In fact, he told Sandra that it would happen one day. Sandra never understood why Drägo didn't consider the possibility that Immigration might take his application for citizenship as a scathing report of a criminal who had learned and practiced his trade on their continent.

Another flurry of activity began. Bill called Sandra asking if he could give her telephone number to an Immigration official. They were trying to drum up a case for deportation and had expressed an interest in talking to her about family violence where Drägo was concerned.

"They can call me if they like, but I really don't know what I can do for them Bill," she said, "I cannot testify against Drägo."

Before Immigration called her, Drägo called asking for her and the kids to testify on his behalf in court. Sandra said she was sorry, but they wouldn't do that. Drägo got angry and wanted to know why not. Sandra said they wouldn't lie in a courtroom if they were asked if they thought he was a reformed criminal. She knew she wouldn't try pretending they were a united family either. Drägo always did that with parole boards and other officials he felt were worthy of deceit. A prison official phoned her one time to set up a conjugal visit. It ended up being denied because Sandra told the fellow that her and Drägo hadn't been living in a common-law relationship before his incarceration.

Sandra told Drägo that Immigration was looking to prove violence in his personal life. He told Sandra that wouldn't pose as a problem because there wasn't any violence to prove. Then Sandra got angry.

"What about the time you beat Steve up for pissing his pants when he was two years old? What about the time when you had me by the throat when the kids were babies? What about the time you were going to punch me through a wall when I was in the wheelchair and the kids stopped you?" she fired the questions at him in a fury.

"I don't know where the hell you get these ideas from!" he shouted at her.

Drägo was furious. Sandra didn't care. She became furious when Drägo said that. According to him, those violent acts never happened. She couldn't believe it.

"You might have forgotten about those incidents, but I sure as hell haven't and never will!" she shouted back.

"Oh, never mind! Just fuck off!" he yelled and hung up the phone.

The time that Drägo was going to punch Sandra while she was sitting in her wheelchair was over an argument over a simple thing that Drägo wouldn't believe. He had been institutionalized for so much of his life that he didn't believe a lot of simple everyday things that happened in the outside world. Things that other people never gave a second thought drove him crazy. On top of that, Drägo had become one of those people who knew everything according to his own estimation. Sandra always wondered how Rumpelstilskin, as she often referred to him, could come out of prison and know absolutely everything about things that he had never seen or dealt with before.

Cruise control on cars scared him. Telephone answering machines mystified him. He refused to believe that a four-cylinder car engine is more economical on gas than an eight cylinder. That was just ridiculous as far as he was concerned. Drägo had never owned a four-cylinder vehicle. Banks infuriated him. He tore a verbal strip off of a teller in a bank one day. Steve was there. Another time in a convenience store Steve watched in disgust and embarrassment as his dad reamed out a young cashier over the price of a package of cigarettes. As Steve told his mother later the poor kid behind the counter was almost bleeding from his nose before Drägo backed off and that the kid had to work for an hour and a half just to be able to afford cigarettes himself. To Drägo, at the time, a job wasn't convenient because it would have interfered with his career. Steve vowed to his mother that he would never go into a store, bank or anything else like it with his father again. It was bullshit for Sandra's doctor to tell her she had arthritis. It was bullshit for Susan's doctor to tell her she had allergies. A "please wait to be seated" sign at an entrance to a restaurant blew Drägo's mind completely. He was going to be served "now," he used to say gritting his teeth. As soon as he saw a sign like that he would leave the establishment infuriated and keep doing that until he found a restaurant without such a "ridiculous" request. He had stood in too many lineups waiting for meals in prison. According to Drägo that self-imposed humiliation gave him the right to have service "immediately" on the outside. Drägo constantly grit his teeth at the slightest of things. The outside world had pissed him off once too often.

One night Sandra was looking at a public notice that had come with the phone bill. Drägo was at her apartment. She commented to Susan that the telephone company had changed their rules so that after the New Year, it would no longer be long distance to call certain places. Sandra proceeded to read aloud the list of places from the public notice in her hand. Rowland Ridge, where the penitentiary was located happened to be one of them. Drägo was listening.

"What are you talking about? It was never long distance to call Rowland Ridge from Riverside," he said.

"Sure it was," Sandra said surprised by his statement and the sudden anger that went with it.

"No, it wasn't!" Drägo said angrily, "I could go back there right now and pick up any phone in the building and call you and it wouldn't be long distance."

"They might well have some direct lines in the offices and places like that, but whenever you called me from there it was always a collect call," Sandra tried to calmly remind him.

"That's because the phones on the ranges don't have any dialers on them. All we could do was pick up the receiver and an operator automatically came on the line." Drägo said through clenched teeth, "The prison just does that to aggravate the inmates."

"Well, whenever I called there to make an appointment to visit it was a long distance call," Sandra said.

Drägo added the telephone company to the list of many, including Sandra, who didn't know what hey were talking about. He continued to adamantly deny that the call was long distance getting more furious as he spoke. Sandra and the kids wondered what was wrong with him. The rage he showed over such a simple thing was unbelievable. Steve got up from his seat then. Sandra could see that he was angry to because of his dad's behavior.

He said, "I'll settle this right now."

He phoned the operator and asked if it was long distance to call Rowland Ridge from Riverside. The operator said it was, but after the first of the year it wouldn't be. Drägo wouldn't listen to any of that. He was still nattering at Sandra. Steve tried handing him the phone to talk to the operator himself, but Drägo wouldn't take the phone. Steve hung up.

Drägo continued to argue black was white but no one was listening anymore. Sandra said nothing more and wheeled herself from the kitchen where the argument started to get away from him. She went and sat in the living room up against a wall saying nothing, pretending to watch TV. Drägo soon followed her still nattering furiously. The kids had little to say in the exasperating conversation because they could see that he was just being plain unreasonable. There was no reasoning with him.

Drägo became vicious because no one wanted to talk about it anymore. In his mind he had a point to prove and Sandra of all people had walked away from him, so to speak. Drägo walked into the living room fuming, grabbed the phone that had a long cord and was on the opposite side of the room from Sandra. He put the phone on her lap and demanded that she call the operator before he stomped back into the kitchen. Sandra sat with the phone in her lap saying nothing as if she was watching TV. She was furious as well, but she was afraid also and contained both of the emotions. Drägo looked at her from the kitchen and went berserk. How dare she ignore him!

He stormed into the living room like a savage and threw the coffee table into a wall embedding it there. The table landed within a foot of Sandra's wheelchair. Drägo grabbed the table and threw it again. It landed upside down half way onto the couch. He bellowed at Sandra to call the "fuckin'" operator. Sandra ripped the cord from the phone and threw the phone on the floor screaming for Drägo to call the "fuckin'" operator himself. She said Steve already had, so why would he believe her.

The next thing Sandra saw was Drägo standing in front of her with a look on his face that she had never seen before. It was the look of murder. He raised his fist as if with the force to punch a brick wall. Susan and Steve jumped on his back screaming at him to stop. He did stop, but was still crazed with anger. Steve got him to leave the apartment. If the kids hadn't been there to stop him he would have definitely gone back to jail then if Sandra survived.

In that fleeting moment with Drägo's fist rose to her that is exactly what she was thinking, ok, this is my excuse to put you back in jail. Then I won't have to work so hard to make sure you do go back. You will have done it all on your own. Go for it.

Sandra shuttered to think that Drägo had shown her a way that would leave her guilt free. He had proven it was a possibility. She wondered when and if she would survive the next outburst that would take place that could rid her family of Drägo.

Sandra recalled the time when Drägo cursed at her on the phone from prison when he hung up the phone denying there had ever been any violence and as much as called her a lunatic. He always thought his calls from the prison were monitored. Maybe they were. He wouldn't admit to anything on the phone that might incriminate him.

Immigration called Sandra two days later after Drägo had hung up on her. The agent asked about family violence. Sandra said there had been because she knew full well that Bill had already mentioned it putting her in a helluva position. The fellow told Sandra that since there was no violence in Drägo's criminal record they had to be able to prove there was in his personal life. He said they might not be able to deport Drägo without her testifying to that. Sandra hoped the man was trying to intimidate her and didn't really mean what he said about not being able to deport Drägo. Why did government departments lean on her so heavily, always stacking the responsibility of Drägo on her shoulders? She told Immigration she couldn't testify unless subpoenaed. Her testimony would have to appear as being involuntarily. Even at that she said they would have to prepare to put her in hiding under the Witness Protection Program because her life wouldn't be worth a wooden nickel. She was afraid of Drägo and made no bones about saying so. Sandra said that Drägo had asked that she testify on his behalf and she had refused. She said he would have killed her on the spot if he could have got his hands on her. She told the man that Drägo was furious with her and had denied the violence she said would come out in court.

Drägo was ordered to be deported a few months later. He would be escorted to Europe on his mandatory release date from prison. He had two years to appeal the decision that he could never step foot on familiar soil again. Bill was the bearer of that information.

Drägo phoned Sandra about that time. He apologized for his reaction on the phone the last time they spoke, but said nothing to indicate what the conversation was about. She vaguely accepted the apology knowing it was his way of admitting she was speaking the truth. He asked her to call his lawyer and speak to him on his behalf. He was appealing Immigration's decision. Sandra said she would call even though she couldn't imagine what that was going to accomplish. Of course she didn't say that to Drägo.

Steve and Sandra both talked to Drägo's lawyer, who specialized in Immigration cases. By the time they got off the phone, they suspected the lawyer didn't have a case to appeal Drägo's deportation. He was surprised to find out that Sandra hadn't lived with Drägo in many years. Drägo had led him to believe that they had lived together until he was imprisoned, that they were a family.

"That man has been in jail for as long as I am old," Steve told the lawyer. "Don't get me wrong, he's my dad and I love him, but I know what he is to."

Steve and Sandra had no idea what Drägo and his lawyer talked about after that. Drägo dropped the appeal process. No one asked why. No one wanted to know.

Drägo's mother spent a considerable amount of time at the prison tutoring him in the foreign language he would be confronted with in Europe. Sandra and the kids went to see Drägo then with his mother. He was happy to see everyone.

Drägo asked Sandra, "What do you think about me being deported?"

"All I know is you don't want to find yourself in a European prison, Drägo," Sandra answered with a foreboding tone in her voice.

She saw a look of fear in his eyes she had never seen before as Drägo digested her warning words.

Drägo called Sandra from Europe several weeks after he settled in as best as he could. Most of his family was there, including his father, so that helped even though he had never met them and was hindered by a language barrier. He told Sandra that government officials had met him at the airport and corralled him for three hours to tell him what a bad boy he was, as Drägo put it. They said they would be keeping a serious eye on him. The only reason that he was there was because his country of origin had no choice but to accept him. The immigration laws had changed from what they had been. Sandra thought about the threat Immigration had often hung over Drägo's head. It was no more than a threat until the law changed.

Before the law was changed, his country of origin could have told Immigration officials, "You raised up that criminal. Now you keep him yourself. We don't want him."

Sandra was emotionally crippled by the guilt she felt. Drägo trusted her with his most precious thing in life, his career.

She couldn't help but think, "Me, of all people to turn him in."

On the day of Drägo's deportation she was in a Crisis Unit owned by the local Salvation Army and staffed with psychiatric nurses. She voluntarily spent two weeks there to receive counseling. It didn't help her guilt because she never said the real reason she was there. It did give her a much-appreciated reprieve from the real world.

Susan and Steve tried reminding her that it was Drägo's own fault that he was deported. They told her she wasn't responsible and that she did what she had to in order save her family. Sandra appeared to be consoled for the kid's sake, but she knew she would never get over the guilt she burdened herself with.

Everyone was sad when Drägo was deported. At the same time they knew that the inevitable had happened. The family struck out to sort their lives now that their lifetime nightmare was finally over.

Chapter Twenty

Two years passed. Drägo called the family occasionally. Steve visited his father in Europe once in that time. It appeared that his dad was keeping his nose clean. He worked seven days a week trying to survive poverty. He worked as a farm hand looking after farm animals. Steve said his father cursed government officials for exiling him. Other than that his spirits were good. Susan got married and had her first child of three. Her husband Luke and Sandra both witnessed the miracle of birth of a beautiful baby girl. Grama cut the umbilical cord. Steve went back to high school and graduated.

Sandra was never at ease again, but wore it well as her doctor said. Before Drägo was deported, she told Bill that if Drägo put his mind to it he could be back on the continent before his escorts were. Bill agreed not doubting her for a second. Both him and Sandra felt that Drägo would be back soon, if not, then later. She heard a news broadcast about a fellow who was deported eighteen times because he just kept coming back.

Sandra always felt like the nightmare would come back to haunt her. She had lived with it for too long to believe that a snap of Immigration's fingers was the cure all. She constantly found herself looking over her shoulder. She became agoraphobic. She feared that when she went out someone from Drägo's past might recognize her. Maybe they knew what she had done. Maybe Drägo had put the pieces together and had asked his criminal friends to do Sandra in. She was horrified that the story might leak out somehow. She felt like her guilt was branded on her forehead. During the seven years that included imprisonment and then deportation, Steve said he didn't think he would ever see his mother laugh again. Susan was concerned about her mother's state of mind as well, fearing Sandra would never be the same. Both kids knew that was true although after several years she had calmed down to a state that was livable. With Drägo on another continent she slowly and cautiously began to feel secure until the war of wits slapped her in the face again.

The dreaded story was told to Steve's employer, a hotel manager. Bill, who Sandra had worked so diligently with and trusted with her life ran off at the mouth like a soup sandwich to Gary, Steve's boss. Bill spotted Steve working in the hotel and asked Gary if he was sure he wanted someone with Steve's history working for him. Gary said he wasn't aware that Steve had a history.

"Oh yes, he does. Him and his mother turned in his dad who the police had chased for many years until he was deported. I was the arresting officer in the end," Bill told Gary as if he was talking about the biggest case of his career.

Gary told Steve what Bill had said. Fortunately, Gary didn't have any security issues where Steve was concerned. That was a blessing because Steve hadn't been working for Gary long at that point. A less reasonable person might have fired Steve on the spot and he would have been none the wiser.

Steve carried the information with him for a month before he told his mother. He knew the hell she had gone through helping the police. He knew the hell his father had put her through most of her life by that time. He feared a yappy cop be the last straw in slipping Sandra's life over the razor's edge of lost control.

Sandra was at Steve's apartment when he ventured, "Mom, Bill told Gary everything about Dad and what we did."

Sandra stared at her son in disbelief. Her mind went into a tailspin.

"Steve, what are you saying?" she questioned him in a level tone.

Sandra really thought she had finally lost her mind and was hearing things at the same time. She knew she had to remain calm. She couldn't risk losing it. She had to get this straight. Either she was hearing things or she was having a nightmare, but she was sure she was wide awake a second before Steve spoke those dreaded words. Then she wondered what she had ever done to her son to deserve becoming the brunt of a deadly joke. Sandra couldn't have heard Steve right. It just couldn't be! Steve repeated exactly what he had said the first time realizing that his mother had quickly retreated into denial.

"Steve, this just can't be! Things like this just don't happen to people, not even us! " Sandra said as though willing Steve to retract what he had told her, making it not true.

"I know, Mom, but they do happen to us," Steve said, wishing with all his heart that the sad fact wasn't true.

Mother and son sat silent for a few seconds looking at each other with sadness in their eyes. They both knew only too well how true that was. Things did happen to their family that others wouldn't see in three lifetimes. They sat in awe pondering that incredible fact. Sandra broke the silence realizing that either one of them could break out in tears of self-pity at any second.

"The whole story?" Sandra asked Steve in utter shock.

"Yes, Mom. The whole story," Steve answered regrettably.

"About the seventy five grand and everything?" his mother asked stupefied.

"Yes, Mom, everything. He even told where the money was and that you took Bill to it," he told her, saddening more as he spoke.

"I can't believe this!" Sandra exclaimed absolutely stunned.

"Neither can I, Mom, but it's true. Gary wouldn't lie to me and there's no way he could have known the story without someone telling him. He knows every detail. Bill and lots of other cops hang out at the hotel.

Steve had kept the devastating story to himself hoping he could protect his mother from the devastation of knowing about it. Finally, he knew he had to tell her. It was her life that was at risk. Drägo's thickly bonded network of criminals wouldn't kill Steve, but they wouldn't think twice about killing Sandra with the word from Drägo. They would kill her in honor of a thief. She was absolutely aghast that the story was out and that it came out of Bill's mouth, of all people. He had a lethal tongue as well.

"What are we going to do, Mom?" Steve asked his mother.

"I don't know yet. I have to think for a minute here. Right this second I only know that Bill cannot get away with this; that's for sure!" Sandra said, pacing the floor.

"I agree, but who are we going to tell? The cops?" Steve asked, snarking at the folly in that.

"No, it won't be the cops that's for damn sure! But I don't know who it will be yet. There has to be somebody we can tell who will do something about this," she told him.

Sandra paced the floor obviously very deep in thought. Steve watched her wondering what was coming next, fearing for his mother's sanity. No one spoke for a few minutes. Sandra kept pacing looking down at the floor. Steve kept watching her mechanical-like movements. Suddenly Sandra stopped pacing and turned toward Steve.

"Call the mayor's office!" she almost yelled to him.

"There's nothing the mayor can do about this, Mom," Steve said disheartened.

Steve thought his mother just might have quietly become emotionally unglued during her pacing. He had hoped she would come up with a better plan of attack than calling a measly mayor.

"I know that," Sandra insisted, knowing how ridiculous the statement sounded even before she said it, "but there's no point in calling the cops to ask who we should call to complain about them. Somebody at the mayor's office will know who we should call."

Sandra knew that official complaints about police officers were usually handled in their Internal Affairs department, but she wanted to make sure that other government officials knew about the devastating news before the cops got a chance to cover it up. Hadn't Bill already proven he couldn't be trusted? Could she trust the police to handle the situation with one of their own? Ears were about to perk up across the country.

Steve headed for the phone glad to know his mother was forming a plan showing she still had her wits about her.

"Just say you want to know who to call to complain about the police. Don't tell them anything else," Sandra warned.

Sandra resumed pacing the floor until Steve got off the phone. She stopped pacing when she heard "Mom." She didn't remember hearing him on the phone at all.

"I have a phone number for a place called the Police Public Complaints Commission (PPCC)," Steve said, bringing Sandra out of a cesspool of thoughts.

"Good! That sounds like the place we need. Give me the number," Sandra said.

She was ready for action. She had been loading her mental cannon during the incessant pacing. Bill had crossed the wrong person. Sandra wouldn't stop until he was as good as crucified. Steve knew that. He was relieved to see that his mother hadn't lost it and had methodically swung into action instead. War had been declared!

"Oh yeah! Hear her roar!" Steve beamed. Throughout his lifetime Steve hadn't always appreciated Sandra's crusading personality. He remembered wishing one time that his mother would quit yakking about the tourists speeding by her driveway. He tried talking Sandra out of a plan she had come up with at the time.

If it hadn't been for rain, Sandra would have spent a Sunday afternoon of one long weekend camped at the thirty-mile speed zone sign across the highway from her home. The highway was the main street of the small town where Sandra lived. It really annoyed her that the tourists didn't take heed of the village speed zone. The general consensus seemed to be that the tourists had just entered a one-horse town so it didn't matter how fast they drove. Sandra was going to sit at the speed zone sign with a sign of her own; telling drivers to slow down because kids lived there to the same as in the city the traffic always sped towards.

Sandra had seen her three-year-old stepbrother hit by a car when she was fifteen. That had made her almost fanatical about kids and traffic. When Susan and Steve were small kids, the family lived in the city in an apartment building. There were many apartment buildings in the area with many young families living in them. The neighbors all complained about a particular driver that sped down the back lane at least twice a day on his way to and from work. Sandra had seen and cursed him but didn't complain to anyone. She just made sure her kids didn't play in the back lane or on the street either for that matter. When she heard others complaining and doing nothing about the speeding driver she decided she was going to put an end to it. No one else wanted to make an effort, they just complained.

Sandra watched in the morning and late afternoon for the fellow to speed down the lane. It took a few days but she soon had his schedule down pat. Taking a shovel in hand she went to the back lane one afternoon when she knew the guy was due to show up. When she heard his car speeding down the lane she stepped from the side of the lane and stood in the middle of it holding the shovel with both hands across the front of her body. The car stopped within a few feet of her. The driver looked at her like she was nuts wondering what was going on. She glared through the windshield at him and then moved to his open car window never letting her eyes leave his. She kept the shovel in the same position.

"What the hell are you doing?" the driver asked her completely bewildered and quite cocky as well.

"Do you see this shovel?" she asked, raising it higher just in case he had missed it.

"Yes. What are you going to do with it?" the man asked, looking frightened.

"Right now I'm not going to do anything with it, but there are lots of kids living in this area," she said calmly.

The fellow looked at her still bewildered as if he was waiting for a punch line but afraid to hear it.

"If you don't slow down when you drive in this alley I'm going to put my shovel right through your windshield," she warned him, adding a threatening tone to her calm voice.

Sandra's eyes didn't leave his. The driver stared at her too stunned to say anything. He appeared convinced that he had encountered a tiny mad woman. He had. The man sat in his car looking at her sheepishly. Sandra didn't move. She kept staring at him waiting for a response.

"I'm sorry," the driver said as if he hardly dared to speak but knew he had to take his turn.

"Ok," was all Sandra said and walked away from the car going to the parking lot of the building she lived in. The man watched her walk away. She didn't look crazy to him anymore.

When Sandra reached the parking lot, she heard the vehicle slowly move on down the back lane behind her. There were no more complaints from the neighbors about the speeding driver because it never happened again. However, at the slightest incident that happened the standard joke in the neighborhood became, "Sandra, where's your shovel?"

Even though Steve didn't always appreciate Sandra's crusades, he was fully aware that there were times in his life when having a crusader as a mother was a good thing. He thought she was a bit like a pit bull. Once Sandra sunk her teeth into something, it was almost impossible to unlatch her. Steve knew he was about to witness another one of those episodes. It would prove to be the crusade of their lifetime in the unrelenting war of wits.

Chapter Twenty-One

Sandra dialed the phone number that Steve had received from the mayor's office. She told a receptionist that answered her call that she needed to speak to someone to file a complaint about the police. The woman asked her to hold the line. Sandra tapped her feet in an attempt to calm herself until a pleasant sounding older man came on the phone asking if he could help her. He had a foreign accent, so Sandra had to listen closely to everything he said. She had never done well with accents.

"I hope you can help me," she said.

"What can I do for you?" the pleasant sounding man asked.

"Before I tell you why I am calling, I want to make sure that I have called the right government office," she said, "What exactly is it that your office does?"

The man told her that he investigated public complaints about the police. Sandra asked if his organization was associated in any way with the police. He said they were not; they were a completely separate entity from the police departments. She questioned him about confidentiality. He assured her that everything was treated with the strictest confidentiality. Files were kept in a locked vault until they were resolved rather than lying around on someone's desk. After resolution, they were destroyed.

Satisfied, but still slightly hesitant, Sandra starting telling the man why she was calling. She told him the important points of her story. The man sounded as if he was astounded before Sandra was finished talking. He asked her questions about what she had told him. She answered his questions.

"Well you people are in danger. Do you want to file a formal complaint?" he asked her sounding concerned.

"Yes, I do," she answered.

"Then put everything you have told me into a letter addressed to me and I will take it from there," he told her about the formality. "You will hear from me soon after I receive the letter. In the meantime, if I were you or your son, I would be very careful and get yourselves a good lawyer."

Sandra thanked him and hung up the phone.

"There that should get the ball rolling," she said to Steve.

"What was the answer when you asked if they had any association with the police?" he asked.

"He said they are a completely different entity, not associated with the police at all," Sandra told Steve.

"Ok, sounds like he's the man we need," Steve said.

After a terrible night of tossing and turning, Sandra put her complaint in writing the next day. She went to the post office and mailed it as soon as she was finished. She wracked her brain wondering what lawyer she should call. Before talking to the man from the PPCC, she was hesitant about talking to a lawyer. Not all of them would be able to handle the case. Not all of them would want to handle the case. She knew she had to find the right one and that probably wouldn't be easy. She needed someone with the experience and the courage to tackle a police force. It would definitely have to be a criminal lawyer. She knew a lawyer that wasn't a criminal lawyer, but had lots of good advice. Sandra did speak to him about it on an informal basis. She appreciated his opinion because he was a straight talker. He told her that the police thought they had eliminated a serious problem when Drägo was deported and that the only problem they had left was her. Although he didn't discourage her crusade, he told her to be careful the cops didn't try eliminating her since she had become a problem to them. Wired for battle, Sandra had a lot of thinking to do.

Sandra got up from a troubled sleep early the next morning. She made coffee and sat down to wait for it to finish dripping with the yellow pages of the phone book in front of her at the kitchen table. It was her favorite place in her home.

When Sandra had bought her house some years earlier, it reminded her of a little farmhouse, but she could see it had the potential to be something different. She didn't believe in little farmhouses. Farmhouses were always big and stately in her mind. The house looked like it begged to be turned into a country cottage style. The kitchen had old grease stained blue and white striped wallpaper on every inch of the walls. Sandra claimed she might go cross-eyed if she had to look at it for long.

Some renovations were done turning the interior of the house into a country style décor, especially the kitchen. It became cozy and warm in appearance with fieldstone and barn board looking paneling and a hard wood floor. A female friend of Sandra's had helped her rip off the old wallboard on a wall behind the stove. They didn't have much to work with in the way of tools, so Sandra went and got the tire iron she always kept under her bed to use as a pry bar. With Sandra standing on the stove and her friend on a stepladder the two women stripped the wall right down to the bare bones. Sandra was ecstatic when she saw what had been covered with wallboard and ancient striped wallpaper. It was wide board planking.

Years later her friend often comments that she will never forget the look on Sandra's face, "Anyone looking at her would have sworn she had just struck gold!"

The sound of the coffee maker gurgling was Sandra's cue that the coffee was ready to drink. She was still in her pajamas and padded around the kitchen in her bare feet getting herself a cup. She took her coffee to the table and sat down with the yellow pages still open in front of her. She scoured the listings for lawyers.

There are a zillion, she thought. *Who is the one who would tackle the police though*?

There has to be someone, she thought just as one name seemed to jump off the page.

"Ah Ha!" she shouted out loud, startling the cat that was laying around, minding his own business for a change.

Sandra made an appointment with the lawyer after telling him her problem in brief. When she got to the man's office, he said he was hoping that an associate—more informed than him—was going to be able to sit in on the meeting. Sandra's hope in the professional immediately deflated. He wasn't her man if he felt he needed help right from the get go. He kept glancing through the glass wall behind Sandra as if he was hoping his buddy would arrive while he talked to her. The lawyer asked her questions about the case. Sandra answered offering as few details as possible, but still getting the idea across. The fellow who sat behind his desk became excited and got more enthused as the meeting went on. At what seemed to Sandra like the peak of his enthusiasm, thinking he had stumbled onto the case that could make his career, he blew it. He told Sandra he would need to do some research to figure out what route he should take admitting he didn't see a case like that come across his desk everyday. He said he would need three thousand dollars to pay for his research.

"You have never seen a case like this come across your desk," Sandra said calmly. "And to boot, you want me to pay you to learn how to proceed with my case. That's just the research part. Once you think you know which way to go you're going to want a huge retainer on top of that. I'll let you know. Thank you for seeing me."

She collected her purse and left his office.

When Sandra got to the front door of the building the lawyer yelled from behind her saying, "Let me know how it works out in any event! I'd be very interested in knowing!"

Sandra glanced over her shoulder acknowledging him and went out onto the street. Her quest for a lawyer had just begun.

Sandra wracked her brain some more until the next day when she remembered a lawyer she had seen years earlier regarding a malpractice suit against a doctor. She didn't file the suit because she didn't want to put her present doctor in a bad situation by asking him to go against one of his colleagues.

This lawyer might be worth a try, she thought.

She called his office only to find out that he had become a judge, but an associate would be happy to see her a receptionist told her.

Sandra walked into the law firm's reception area two days later. A tall burly looking man soon greeted her. He introduced himself as Tod Waterton and showed her into his office. While Sandra was telling him her story he got excited and agitated at the same time. He looked alarmed.

"Well, you need the Witness Protection program, Sandra!" he told her as he got up out of his chair. "Excuse me, I will be right back!

Sandra thought, *Oh no, he's running for help already, but at least he can see the graveness of the situation. I guess I just have to realize that anyone who takes this case is going to be consulting with other associates because most lawyers have not run across this situation before. He seems to be somewhat on the ball though.*

Sandra waited about five minutes before Tod came back. He didn't appear agitated anymore but he was no less excited. They talked at great length. The Witness Protection Program didn't come back into the conversation that day. Sandra gave Tod a newspaper article about Drägo when he had hit the top ten-wanted list. She showed him the one about the loot as well and gave him a copy of the complaint she had written.

Before she left his office Tod promised Sandra that he would get right on the case. He said he had some priorities at the time but would lay them aside to work on her case because of the urgency he felt about it.

About a week later Sandra received a letter from the PPCC. The letter said her complaint had been filed and there would be an investigation started immediately.

Tod called Sandra and said the police department Internal Affairs and Witness Protection departments had requested a meeting with her and Steve in his office.

"Why?" Sandra asked him.

"Because they are investigating your complaint!" he said as if he could hardly believe she had asked.

Sandra agreed to a date. At the same time she was annoyed. The PPCC fellow had led her to believe that his office would be the investigators. He hadn't confirmed her belief that the police does their own investigating into complaints about one of their own. Sandra could see the futility in that. The man had told her that his office was a completely separate entity. Sandra thought she had made herself very clear over the telephone about not wanting the police involved. She wasn't impressed at all. Had the pleasant sounding man deliberately mislead her and if so why? The situation made her think of how ludicrous it was to ask doctor to fight doctor, lawyer to fight lawyer and cop to fight cop. Sandra found out months later that the PPCC office is partially staffed by some former police officers. The thought of a meeting with Internal Affairs was ridiculous to her, but she would go if for no other reason than to let them know that they couldn't intimidate her.

Sandra and Steve arrived at Tod's office on the agreed upon date and time. Tod was already talking to the police in a boardroom. The room was right off the reception area where the son and mother sat down. The door to the boardroom was ajar. The mother and son could hear their lawyer and the officials talking and laughing although they couldn't make out anything that was said. They looked at each other and had one of their silent conversations that didn't require words.

Had either one spoke, it would have been to say, "Don't they sound buddy-buddy in there."

Steve was the first to go into the boardroom to be interviewed. The authorities were attempting to prove their status and control by insisting on interviewing the two people separately. Both Steve and his mother knew that was an intimidation tactic cops always use. Neither one was fazed or surprised by it.

At one point the door to the interview room opened while Steve was in there and Tod went to get a glass of water for Steve. He told his mother later that he had been yelling so loud that his voice got hoarse. Tod had to intervene like a referee between Sergeant Drake from Internal Affairs and Steve a couple of times when things got too heated.

Among other things Steve told the police was that Sandra had become a psychiatric mess. Drake asked Steve what his mother's reaction had been to hearing the dreaded story. He told the sergeant that her reaction was absolute utter shock; she had literally trusted Bill with her life, her physical existence, with her children's physical existence and her mental health. Steve went on to say that between working with the police against Drägo and Bill telling the story, his mother had been destroyed.

When asked if his mother and father were in a relationship at the time Sandra worked with the police, Steve told Drake that they were not. He said that Sandra had tried several times to be in a family relationship with his father but couldn't do it. He also said if it were not for Drägo's career, his mother and father would have been together forever. Sandra was glad to know that her son knew those things. She felt sure he did but she had never known him to speak of it.

When Steve's interview was over he joined his mother in the reception area where she was waiting. He spoke to Sandra in hurried hushed tones.

"They're using tape recorders. They are hammering on the fact that you changed your last name. They have something they want you to sign as well.

"Don't sign anything, Mom," Steve said to her quickly with a warning look. "I'm not signing anything. I know what they are trying to do. Not to worry!" Sandra said smiling, assuring Steve.

Steve caught the dual meaning of what his mother was saying to him. He had been concerned about how she would hold up under fire. Sandra felt his concern and let him know that she wasn't going to be coerced into anything and she had her full wits about her. She knew what it would be that Internal Affairs wanted her to sign. Her internal cannon was loaded. Then Sandra's presence was requested in the boardroom.

Immediately after the formality of introductions were over, Sergeant Drake slid a legal sized piece of paper across the table putting it in front of Sandra. At the same time he said he would appreciate it if she signed the paper. She glanced at the document. It was a document that would informally release the police force from the complaint she had against them. She knew it would absolve them from responsibility and any further proceedings on the matter as well. Sandra's icy glare looked directly into Drake's eyes.

"You can bet I won't be signing this," she said as she folded the paper putting it into a small black case she carried.

Sandra held her ground. She wouldn't waiver from her belief that a yappy disgraceful cop had put her life in danger.

One of the first questions Drake asked her was what her working relationship with Bill was like. She lied saying it was excellent. Her experience with Bill had left some things to be desired, leaving her to wonder about his competence. She didn't think the interview was the time or place to bring up any of the moves Bill had made that she thought were stupid. That would have made her appear to be a petty woman, hindering her credibility. She wanted everyone in the room to know that she was just as serious as the situation at hand. She couldn't help but think she wouldn't have been sitting there if she had put up with Randy's by the book routine and his mistrustful attitude toward her. He would have gone strictly by the book and not run off at the mouth with her story, as if it was his biggest case ever. Sandra didn't bother to mention the fact that she had refused to work with Randy. Everyone in the room would have known that already. Mention of that would have come across as petty as well. She asked if Bill thought there was a statutory limit of seven years on his duty as a police officer to keep his informant's identities confidential. Drägo had spent five years in prison before he was deported two years earlier.

Sandra only fought when she knew she was dead right or to protect her kids when they needed protecting. She wasn't a mother who believed that her kids could do no wrong. She always held her children accountable for their own actions from a very young age. When they were adolescents she made them accountable for their friends' actions in the family home as well. She wouldn't tolerate being told, "so and so did it" when something had been done wrong in the household when the kid's friends had been visiting while she was absent.

The mother remembered a particular summer when her children were five and six years old. The family had just moved onto a residential street that ran several blocks between two major arteries in the city. There was a school less than a block from their home on the same street. The kids liked to go there and play on the swings and other playground equipment. One afternoon they had both come home from the schoolyard shortly after they had gone there. Sandra asked why they were back home so soon. The kids told her that a "bigger" girl had told them they couldn't play at the school. The girl had harassed them until they left.

A few days later Susan's bike was stolen. She told her mother that the girl from the schoolyard had taken it. Sandra asked where the girl lived. Susan told her. Sandra walked down the back lane with both of her kids until she got to the girl's house. A hefty woman was standing by the garage on the property. Sandra said nothing to her. The garage door was open. Sandra saw Susan's bike in the garage.

She walked past the woman, walked into the garage, wheeled Susan's bike out, walked past the woman again and said, "This is my daughter's," tossing a defiant look at the large woman.

The woman glared at her but didn't say a word.

The next day the kids went to play at the schoolyard after protesting that the "bigger girl" would be after them again. Sandra told them to go ahead and play but if they encountered any problems with the girl they were to let her know. A few minutes later the kids came home crying. The girl was at the schoolyard. She had been very nasty and threatened them by saying, "I will kick both of you in the ass if I ever see you here again!"

That was it. Sandra walked to the schoolyard fuming. She spotted the girl who was about ten years old with long dark hair and walked straight toward her with a menacing look on her face. The kids had given her a description of the girl. She asked the girl what her name was. The girl told her rather defiantly but with a hint of fear that her name was Tammy.

"Well, Tammy, my kids keep coming home telling me that you won't let them play here. So I am here to tell you that if you don't leave them alone, I will take you by your long hair and drag you from Ward Street to Silver Street and back again!" Sandra's tone was threatening.

The girl looked horrified, but tried valiantly to hold her own. Sandra couldn't help but admire her courage.

"I'm going to get my mother! She's bigger than you are!" Tammy shouted at Sandra.

"You do that because I'd like to talk to your mother too, and it's no matter how big she is!" Sandra said and walked away.

The next day the kids went to play at the schoolyard with encouragement from their mother. They played there for an hour or so, and reported to Sandra when they got home that Tammy had been nice to them and had even played with them. Sandra smiled. The kids continued to go to the schoolyard regularly encountering no further problems. One afternoon they were gone for quite some time before they came home with Tammy behind them. The three kids looked like they had been friends forever.

Tammy looked at Sandra warily when the kids invited her into their home. Sandra saw the girl's hesitation and invited the girl in herself. Tammy said "Hi" to Sandra rather shyly. Sandra smiled and returned the greeting as if she was meeting the girl for the first time. Tammy spent a lot of time at the home during the remainder of the summer. She ended up proving that she could be as nice as she could be nasty. Sandra could relate to that. Tammy often talked to Sandra while the two sat around the kitchen table. Sandra had always got along with kids because she treated them like the little people they are. She often smiled to herself during conversations with Tammy wondering if the girl had come to visit her or her kids. It got a bit out of hand though and became obvious that the little girl wasn't there to play with Susan and Steve. She started consuming Sandra's time whenever she was around which was almost every day. Sandra finally had to tell Tammy politely that she should go and play with the kids. Tammy did. She wasn't offended.

Throughout their lives Sandra's kids, their friends and her could often be found sitting around the kitchen table having great conversations. Some chats were very serious. Others were downright comical.

Sandra got along well with everyone from every age group and every walk of life unless they became a serious problem to her or her kids. In that event, the mother's scorn kicked in with full throttle although she was a very patient woman. It took a lot to rattle her. Sandra seldom reacted to a bad situation on impulse. Every thought she had when faced with a bad situation was carefully thought out, all be it maybe in a split second, because as she often said herself she had to learn to think before she spoke. Even at that her lethal tongue could lash out at anyone she thought deserving of a good lashing. Sandra always said her only defense was her mouth. As an adult, one of Steve's friends since childhood laughed after seeing Sandra in a verbal altercation with a crazed woman.

He said, "I just about bust up laughing when you turned on her because I knew you wouldn't listen to much more from her. I was just waiting to see when you were going to pounce. In all the years I have known you I have never known you to back down from anyone."

Sandra's interview with Internal Affairs went on for about an hour. Drake asked Sandra about her last name wanting to know why she had changed it. She sensed he was fishing hoping that she would inadvertently say something that would reveal some dark reason for the change. Sandra appreciated Steve's message in the reception area because she had never dreamt her name would be an issue. She had even forgotten about it. She learned later through some investigation of her own that Drake had gone to considerable trouble to find out whom the little demon was who dared to take on the police force. He had checked her out thoroughly hoping he could get something on her that would shut her up. Her last name had posed as a problem in the sergeant's investigation. The motor vehicle branch did a search at Drake's request for women by the name of Sandra in the small community where she lived. Sandra was the only woman by that first name. Then he went to the local police station where Sandra lived. The sergeant there said he knew Sandra by a different last name and that her house was listed for sale. Armed with that information Drake hoped to find incrimination regarding the change of name, discrediting her. Neither of Sandra's last names revealed anything he could discredit her with. Sandra was humored to know that Drake had been mystified and had gone to such lengths over her identity. After all, she had told Bill that she had changed her last name. Sandra always marveled over the lack of communication in government departments, particularly in police departments.

Drake was quick to point out the fact that Sandra received the information about Bill's alleged improper disclosure of information as third hand information. He asked if anyone else was present during the conversation between the hotel manager and Bill. Sandra said fortunately there wasn't and pointed out that a witness would have made matters worse. Another person would have known her deadly secret. Drake was insinuating that because Sandra got the information third hand and there was no witness to the conversation she didn't have a case against Bill. Sandra pointed out to him that conversations between two people are often not witnessed.

"If there are the only two people in a room, how the hell could there possibly be a witness?" she asked him, receiving no answer.

She knew about another conversation between the manager and cop that hadn't been witnessed either. Bill had gone to Gary's office when the shit hit the fan and asked him why he would do such a thing to him. Gary responded telling Bill that he was a straight shooter and believed that what Bill had done was wrong. Bill complained to Gary saying he could lose his job over it. Gary told him that was his own doing and no one else was to blame. Another police officer who congregated at the hotel knew what Bill had done, somehow. He told Gary that Sandra and Steve should "nail him to the cross" because he had always been a yappy cop and talked about Drägo's investigation often. If Sandra hadn't wondered how many people Bill had told before she heard that she certainly wondered then.

The officer from the Witness Protection program took his turn at asking Sandra questions. He didn't see any reason why Sandra should think she was in any kind of danger. He told her if something happened to the contrary in the future she should let him know.

"Isn't that a bit like putting up lights at a railroad crossing after it's deemed that enough people have been killed?" Sandra asked, her glare ever present. "I had a man tell me one time that he would burn my house down. I had no reason to believe that kind of insane statement. He came back the next day and did it. You can check this out with the Blainsworth police department if you like. He also had an audiotape delivered to that station saying he was going to kill himself and then me. He did kill himself. I didn't happen to be home. That's the only reason I am here to tell the story today. So I should just wait until someone threatens my life again? Is that what you're saying?"

No one responded. The meeting was brought to a close unless Sandra had something more to add Drake announced. She did.

She read from a prepared statement she had written. Her concentration was seriously impaired by the stress of the breech so she knew she had to write things down that she wanted to say.

"The day that Drägo was deported, I was in a Crisis Unit run by the Salvation Army and spent a little over two weeks there. On two other occasions I was admitted to Blainsworth hospital, first, a suicide attempt, and the second, a nervous breakdown. I have since been diagnosed with a mood disorder that causes extreme fluctuations in chemical balance in a matter of minutes. I have been on a myriad of psychiatric medications and sleeping pills for the past couple of years, suffering from severe depression and agoraphobia. Counseling in those years has offered some relief, but I still suffer in my personal relationships. Everyday things such as shopping or going out in public in general are real accomplishments for me as I constantly feel like I should be looking for people who might know me. These fears have been getting constantly worse since my dealings with the police. Bill said if he could ever do anything for me I was to let him know. Well there is something he can do for me: he can get rid of my fear of the police and their connections. He can restore my morals that had me hell bent on stopping the one-man crime spree Drägo lived. He can let me believe that there is such a thing as confidentiality again. He can promise the safety of my family and myself. He can take another job where loose lips are not detrimental to peoples lives, and lastly he can get the hell out my nightmares. If Bill can accomplish all of the above, then he will never see my face again. If not, then he will soon see that he has pissed of the wrong lady. Stupidity is not illegal, but I believe that putting someone's life in danger is."

"Sandra we're sorry to hear about your health condition, but would a meeting with Bill and a personal apology interest you?" Drake asked, dismissing anything else she had said.

"Don't even think about it! I never want to see that man's face again!" she nearly shouted. "Can you tell me why you are trying so hard to get me to listen to an apology when you keep telling me there has been no wrong done? The last time I looked an apology is an admission of guilt! I will chase that man right to the highest court in the land if that's what it takes! I will not let him get away with this! I will fear for my life for the rest of it, and you folks are trying to get away with a little embarrassment. How dare you?"

Tod was the only person in the room who had any comments about what Sandra had said. He said he wasn't sure that there wasn't a criminal charge against Bill for putting lives in danger by the telling of the story. The meeting came to an abrupt end. Then Tod asked to have a copy of the recorded meeting. Drake assured him that he would prepare a copy for him and put it in the mail.

Sandra joined Steve in the reception area. They walked out of the building even more hell bent on crucifying Bill. His superiors would find themselves caught in the line of fire since they had chosen to put themselves on the front line. So be it.

Chapter Twenty-Two

Before the meeting with Internal Affairs, Tod did some intense work on Sandra's behalf. She was happy to have finally found someone who could and would tackle the police. He insisted her local police department patrol her residence regularly because no one knew how far or to whom the entire story had leaked. The local department had no idea why they were instructed to patrol by her home, apparently and according to a Police Inspector. Sandra had moved out of her own home and put it up for sale due to fear for her life. She stayed in the house for some months that the police were patrolling and then moved into Riverside. Could she trust the rural police? If she needed help, she wanted to be able to call Riverside city police and not the police force she was waging war with. Sandra chuckled when she was first considering that move. Surely she would never run into the city police officers that she had told to get to hell out of her apartment years before. Since they were more than beat cops they would never be responding to a 911 call. Still the thought of moving back into their jurisdiction lent some humor to the dire situation.

Several months passed. In the meantime Sandra never knew what was going to happen next. She came to expect everything and anything. Tod backed away as her lawyer. He sent her a letter telling her that his schedule didn't allow for the time and dedication her case needed. He also stated that she should find other legal council or carry on with the case by herself. Sandra took that letter to a large criminal law firm in Riverside. Mitch, a lawyer there sympathized but told her the letter was exactly what she had suspected. Had police intimidation finally worked with Tod? Through some investigation of her own under the

Privacy Act Sandra discovered later that Tod was acquainted with Bill on some level.

"You realize that anyone taking on this case will be putting themselves and their family at risk," Mitch said.

"So, what you're telling me is that there isn't a lawyer in Riverside who will take on this case just because we're dealing with the police," Sandra said.

Mitch said on the contrary that he would love to take on the case, but Sandra couldn't afford the large retainer he required.

It took a year before Sandra got a response through the PPCC about her complaint against the law enforcement agency. Sergeant Drake, who was assigned the investigation, responded after what he considered a thorough investigation. Simply put, he claimed that because there was no witness to the conversation between Gary and Bill he didn't find her complaint valid. Drake also stated that Sandra was free to appeal the findings of his investigation.

In a heart beat, she thought as she re-read the letter from Internal Affairs.

She appealed her case to the Police Commission who came up with the same result except for one paragraph in their letter. That one paragraph said that "however" in any event the story should have never been told. That's what the hell Sandra had been saying all along.

While Sandra appealed and waited for the "however" in the investigation she called everyone from an agency that investigates law enforcement to Human Rights to no avail. For weeks the telephone book lay open to the gray pages of the government telephone listings. She often called organizations just to find out what they did because telephone listings do not always make an organization's purpose obvious. Some government offices would refer her to one that in turn referred her back to the original one. Sandra was going in circles and getting nowhere. Regardless, she plodded on, recording every conversation. Ninety-minute audiotapes full of telephone conversations began piling up. She couldn't help but think about how well the police department's butts were covered.

When she called the Department of Justice, looking for justice, a soft female voice said, "We defend the police."

"Oh, so what you are saying is that we would be on the opposite side of the bench in a court room," Sandra said with a hint of humor.

"That's right," the pleasant woman told her, "but good luck to you."

Sandra was determined that there had to be someone out there who would help her. She paced incessantly back and forth between her kitchen and living room when she didn't have the phone book on her lap. Steve watched a lot of that. He was afraid for his mother's sanity because her crusade was coming up empty.

"There has to be somebody that I have missed," Sandra insisted to Steve.

"I think you've called everybody south of God, Mom," Steve said, wishing his mother would give up but knowing she wouldn't.

Sandra ignored what Steve had said but laid her plan down momentarily that day. She put the phone book away for appearance sake. She was aware that she looked like a crazed woman. It was all right to be crazed when she was alone but not with a loved one watching.

Sandra got up the next morning still in crusade mode. She was home alone so there was no one there to think she had lost it. She got a cup of coffee and retrieved the phone book. It lay in her lap as she scanned the government listings again seeing all the numbers she had already called. Sandra ignored the fleeting feelings of defeat that insisted on nagging her.

Suddenly she yelled aloud, "Yes! How could I have missed this?"

"How stupid of me!" she scolded herself. "I've just about driven myself nuts for the past weeks and it was right under my nose all along."

She was very excited. A name and phone number seemed to have jumped off the page in front of her like a slap in the face. It was for The Commission of Privacy. Sandra took a few minutes to collect herself, containing her excitement, before she dialed the number. She couldn't come off as the near lunatic she feared she might have become.

It wasn't long before Sandra knew she had finally called the right people. The woman she spoke to was very concerned about Sandra's story and told her to put her complaint in writing and mail it to her. Another official complaint went into the mail system.

Before long Sandra was excited and hopeful when she received an envelope in the mail from The Commission of Privacy. The Commission planned a trip to Riverside to investigate the complaint. The officials would be interviewing all involved including Gary, Bill and Internal Affairs. One of two officials to arrive was familiar with the tactics of the police force and how those tactics were used to try and weasel their way out of everything. Sandra was elated.

The agents from the Commission of Privacy arrived in Riverside during that bitter cold winter. After a day or two of interviews they claimed Sandra's complaint was "well founded."

With information obtained under the Privacy Act from the Police Commission, Sandra learned that the police were concerned about the powers of the Privacy organization among other concerns. Faxes, memos and emails flew back and forth across the country between departments of the police. Everyone from Chief Staff Sergeants, Commanding Officers and constables was involved in the fight against Sandra to save one of their own.

Sandra had problems obtaining her own personal information from the police under the Privacy Act. The police didn't want her to have it because that information would pass on hints as to what they were thinking. They stalled, and hoped Sandra would just go away. Finally, after a screaming match with an official from the Police Commission, and involving the Privacy agents again, Sandra received about two hundred pages of heavily censored information about her case. At least one quarter of the paper pile was censored. That didn't bother Sandra because what wasn't wiped out gave her a good insight as to what the authorities were thinking.

Tod never did get a copy of the taped interview with Internal Affairs. Sandra demanded her own copy and got it after a lot of hassle. First Witness Protection claimed Internal Affairs had the tape. Next Internal Affairs claimed Witness Protection had it. Then both departments tried pacifying Sandra with a typed transcript. She insisted on having a copy of the tape as well. Do the police hate giving up information or what? Of course the transcript and audiotape were censored as well. Sandra didn't care. She demanded the tape because it was her right to have it.

It was her way of letting the law know that she knew her rights and would act upon them. She knew enough from the paper pile that she had the police right where she wanted them. They were damned concerned knowing she wasn't about to just go away as they wished she would. Their obstinacy, deliberately making every move she made difficult, drove Sandra harder to make sure they didn't get away with covering up an offence of one of their own.

Through all that Sandra still didn't have legal counsel. Knowing that seasoned professionals had been and could be intimidated by the police Sandra decided to try a rookie, if for no other reason, than advice. Someone not officially involved with the legal system could hold potential important information. She made an appointment with a paralegal, John. Steve went to the meeting with her. John became more intrigued as Steve and Sandra spoke. John's wife who was a nurse lurked in the wings listening to everything. Sandra didn't care for that but after all she was in the woman's home. The story unfolded in John's living room. He proved to be full of interest and information. Sandra and Steve went away feeling quite good about the meeting. John promised to investigate some things for them and to keep in touch.

Sandra and John spoke on the telephone a few days later. John was still gung-ho about the situation. Over the next two or three weeks Sandra left several messages for John to call her. None of the calls were returned. Finally John's wife answered the phone one day and told Sandra that her husband was an epileptic who had been bedridden for the past weeks. Sandra wondered how stupid she looked that she should believe a nurse telling her that an epileptic was bedridden from his condition. Epilepsy wasn't the problem.

"What the fuck is that?" Sandra exclaimed as she walked into her home a few days before the meeting with John.

She had just returned home after being away for several hours. While driving from one end of the city to the other, she had noticed a car following her. It disappeared while she went into a convenience store on her route, but was right on her tail again on the freeway. There were two women in the car that followed Sandra until she turned down a short street that would take her directly home.

When Sandra unlocked her back door, she noticed that about a ten-inch length of heavy gauge weather stripping was torn out of its slot in the area of the lock. The thick rubber was scarred with several screwdriver marks. No one was in the house. Everything was in place just as Sandra had left it. Nothing was missing. It wasn't an average break in. It was the day after she had a heated discussion with the Police Commission over the telephone about not receiving her private information in a timely manner.

Sandra wondered, *is there any point to calling the police on the police*?

She did make a phone call reporting the incident, but not to the police. She reported it to her leasing office and property manager to have a record of it. She knew full well that her conversation with the office was being monitored. She wanted the police to be aware that she was aware.

The following day Steve and Sandra set a mini trap for anyone entering the house while they were both away. The trap was undetected and set off. The intruders were not as sloppy as they had been the day before. Sandra noticed that she wasn't able to access the Internet any longer though. She had her computer completely taken apart and checked out by a technician who found nothing. The bugging equipment the police installed in her home on their first visit was removed on the second visit as legal council said it would be. Sandra deliberately told Steve the night before that she was going to have the place scanned for bugs. Next she called her Internet provider.

After a bit of troubleshooting, Sandra said, "Just say for example someone was listening to this conversation we're having right now, would that be the cause of instantly being spit off the net?"

"Oh, for sure," the technician said. "The telephone line is too small to handle that kind of interference."

After John had been frightened off, Sandra had found a lawyer who wasn't intimidated by law enforcement. He was in fact in the process of suing one of the members regarding a personal case against him. The case was all over the news when Sandra was still wracking her brain as to where she was going to find legal council. After listening to a radio news broadcast regarding the case, mentioning the lawyer's name, Sandra called him. She had fought for months on her own.

An appointment with the lawyer, Bruce, was arranged. He was gung-ho like the rest had been. When Sandra finished with most of the details, Bruce told her he would need a large retainer. When Sandra said she didn't have that kind of money, Bruce bid for the job coming down to a small retainer that she could afford.

A meeting with a Department of Justice lawyer and the Witness Protection Program again was soon scheduled but to no avail. However, within a day Sandra was able to access the Internet again after she let the officials know that after the home invasion and because of the Internet she was aware of a tap on her telephone line.

Sandra held her ground. Steve stood firm with her during the interview. It was a lot of the same bullshit repeated. The general consensus was that no one had threatened Sandra's life and the police believed the breech had been contained. None of that mattered to Sandra because she had believed her story was contained for seven years in protected files in the bowels of a federal building. Those files didn't even contain her name. She was a number and should have remained so. Ignoring his oath to secrecy, Bill had broken the most sacred of all law enforcement agencies, informant privileges. Sandra distinctly remembered him telling her that she couldn't even trust another police officer with the information. She had thought that statement was a bit rash when he said it. Apparently not. Bill, of all people, was the last one Sandra would have thought to prove that statement true.

A lawsuit was filed against Bill and his superior governing body. Again, Sandra's name wasn't mentioned. The Chief Justice Minister granted her anonymity because the particulars of the case would identify her. The suit was also put into the courts as a sealed document to prevent public access such as the media. Earlier in the memos, faxes and other correspondence between the police officials it was mentioned that there was no media attention as yet. It was stated that no dollar figure amount had been stated yet as well and that Sandra's lawyer was a litigation lawyer. It was also mentioned that the complaint had the potential for adverse media attention.

Bruce sued for a half a million dollars. Sandra and the lawyer signed a contingency agreement that would give him forty percent of that. One day under the eighteen-month limit the suit was filed. Sandra was back in the Crisis Unit for refueling and reloading her mental cannon.

The admitting nurse said to Sandra, "It's a good thing that you brought documentation of your claim with you. Otherwise I would have thought that you are not well enough to be here."

Sandra knew what that meant. She had seen others transferred to the local psychiatric hospital. Sandra took papers with her to prove her story because a psychiatrist had doubted her before that and verified the bizarre story of her home being broken into and other events with Steve. It so happened that Steve was waiting for Sandra in the waiting room of the psychiatrist and was asked in to verify parts of the story.

Susan and Steve shook their heads often when they used to say, "There are many things that have happened in our lives that there is just no point in telling anyone, because no one will believe us when they hear these fantastic stories coming out of the mouths of people who just end up sounding like liars."

Life carried on. Sandra quietly waited for a come back from the police department. She assumed they had eighteen months to respond since she had eighteen months to sue. Not so. Sandra found out later that the law enforcement agency only had twenty-one days to respond. Bruce said nothing. In her stressed out state, the woman had missed the twenty-one day information on some papers that her lawyer had given her. Sandra called him almost eighteen months to the day of the suit being filed. During a meeting with him, Bruce told Sandra that because a year and a half had passed and she hadn't had any threats on her life he was inclined to agree with the police. No one felt that her life was in danger. She reminded Bruce that she had thought that for seven years until Bill opened his mouth.

At the same time Bruce dictated a letter to the Department of Justice lawyer asking for a settlement of twenty thousand dollars and saying he hoped the matter could be cleared up in the next few months allowing three months in total. Sandra's signature on a form gave Bruce permission to write the letter and said that she agreed with the terms.

Sandra called Bruce, as instructed, a few weeks later when he expected to have an unofficial response from the Department of Justice.

"Oh yes, Sandra, hold the line please, I'll put you right through," Bruce's secretary said brightly.

Sandra waited for a few minutes on the line. The secretary came back on the telephone.

"I'm sorry, Bruce is in a meeting. Can I put you through to his voice mail?" the secretary asked with the brightness gone out of her voice.

"Sure you can," Sandra said dryly.

She left a message reminding Bruce that he had told her to call at that time. She knew he was a busy man, but was he too busy to respond to her call? Apparently. He didn't respond. Was he in bed with the Department of Justice or had he lost interest because there was no money in it anymore?

Sandra didn't want the twenty thousand dollars. Sandra didn't want the half a million dollars. All she ever wanted was the police to admit that Bill had breeched his duty as a police officer and to see him punished for his blatant disregard for her safety. A settlement would have been an admission of guilt, but Sandra knew that if she accepted any offer she would have to sign a confidentiality agreement. She would never sign such a thing. Did the cops actually expect her to be a party to a law enforcement cover-up?

The legal time limit that Sandra agreed to has expired. She smiles to herself when she thinks about the fact that Bruce and the police think she has just gone away. Five years after the breech of information Sandra has gone away, but not as officials hoped.

When Bill goes to work now, he drives the highways in a patrol car and wears a uniform. The best advice a lawyer ever gave Sandra was that she should write a book.

Gotta go now cause I hear Hollywood calling.

Printed in the United States
23943LVS00004B/97-126